"Kiss me." Kyle touched his forehead to Alice's, repeated the incredible words, with his voice so husky it sent shivers across her skin. "Kiss me."

"That's—that's n-not—"

His hands closed around her upper arms. Holding her as if he'd never let go.

She shut her eyes. Her knees were giving out. "You can't do this. You can't kiss me."

"I can."

"No." She stared at him—boldly. Perspiration stung her eyes. With a supreme effort she battled back the heady whirl of being admired, sought, wanted. "I couldn't do that. Company policy, isn't it? What's wrong for your staff is wrong for you, too."

Kyle's surprise gave her a slim opening. She spun and jammed the key into the lock, then slammed the door behind her without looking back because she wasn't at all certain that she shouldn't have kissed him exactly as he'd wanted.

Damn the consequences…

Dear Reader,

Who wouldn't love to have *A Holiday Romance*? There's something magical about the thought of being swept away by romance and adventure while on vacation from your everyday world. What better time to have a fantasy come true?

A Holiday Romance is the companion book to last year's *Nobody's Hero,* which was the story of the man who stayed at Alice Potter's island cottage. This time, Alice gets her turn at a luxury Arizona resort. After years of putting her dreams on hold in order to give to others, Alice is determined to finally find her own adventures, even if that means stepping out of her comfort zone and into a desert monsoon. Along the way she also lands a romantic hero. Maybe even two of them!

On holiday, almost anything can happen....

XOXO,

Carrie Alexander

P.S. To see more of Alice's postcards home, visit me on the Web at www.carriealexander.com, where you can also find my backlist, drop me a line and perhaps enter for my latest giveaway.

A HOLIDAY ROMANCE
Carrie Alexander

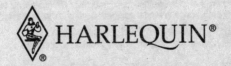

HARLEQUIN®

TORONTO • NEW YORK • LONDON
AMSTERDAM • PARIS • SYDNEY • HAMBURG
STOCKHOLM • ATHENS • TOKYO • MILAN • MADRID
PRAGUE • WARSAW • BUDAPEST • AUCKLAND

Recycling programs
for this product may
not exist in your area.

ISBN-13: 978-0-373-71567-1

A HOLIDAY ROMANCE

This edition published by arrangement with Harlequin Books S.A.

ABOUT THE AUTHOR

Carrie Alexander considers every book she reads a mini-vacation, although she admits that writing them is not! A prolific author and two-time RITA® Award finalist, Carrie lives year-round in her own vacation wonderland in the north country of Upper Michigan. Between deadlines and home improvement projects, she sometimes gets to enjoy it.

Books by Carrie Alexander

HARLEQUIN SUPERROMANCE
1042—THE MAVERICK
1102—NORTH COUNTRY MAN*
1186—THREE LITTLE WORDS*
1239—A FAMILY CHRISTMAS*
1408—A READY-MADE FAMILY*
1455—A TOWN CALLED CHRISTMAS
1504—NOBODY'S HERO

*North Country Stories

SWAP YOUR VACATION HOUSE AT
HOLIDAYS AWAY!

Available July 21-Aug 3, Prince Montez Oasis Resort, near Phoenix, Arizona: luxurious two-bedroom condo with all the amenities. Air-conditioning, private spa, garden tub with walk-in shower. Full access to resort activities, including golf, tennis, horseback riding and adventure sports. Fine dining, boutiques, night clubs. Last-minute listing—enjoy romance under the desert stars with this rare offer!

CHAPTER ONE

AN EXPERIENCED traveler would have known better.

Alice Potter scolded herself as she trekked up the wide stone steps of the grand hotel, panting and perspiring copiously even though the temperature had dropped since her arrival that afternoon. The walk from her quarters to the center of the resort had been longer and hotter than she'd expected.

July in Arizona! Most people—the *smart* ones—had fled north for the season. What had she been thinking?

The answer was simple. She'd been desperate to get far away from Maine. To a land of cactus and sunshine, where she could lose her old self like a snake shedding its skin. She'd expected that she would be someone different in Arizona. Someone unapologetically *alive.*

She licked her salty upper lip. "Bi-i-ig mistake."

But was it?

"Ma'am?" prompted the doorman, a clean-cut fellow with apparently no sweat glands beneath his peaked cap and starched white coat. He'd opened the immense double doors, hand-carved slabs of wood inset with grids of glass framed by rustic black iron.

Alice thanked him and stepped inside.

The spacious lobby was an intimidating dazzle of

light and activity. She paused to swipe a hand across her forehead, wishing she'd thought to bring a handkerchief. Surreptitiously she rubbed her palm on the flouncy fiesta skirt she'd purchased online. The white cotton eyelet top that exposed her indoor-pale arms and shoulders was already sticking to her skin.

She'd envisioned her arrival differently—a carefree stroll through a cool lobby populated by potted palms and lean, dark, mysterious men. Casablanca glamour by way of Phoenix luxury resort.

Instead, she was…well, she was still herself.

Nervous, uncertain, alone, and now sweaty, too.

But God bless central air. She sucked in a deep breath, thinking longingly of home. The fresh salt breeze that washed over the island, the cool shade of the sheltering pines. On Osprey Island, they didn't need air-conditioning, even in summer.

For the past six years of her mother's illness, Alice had rarely been off the island. Swapping Pine Cone Cottage for a two-week stay at a desert resort condo had been the first whim she'd indulged in in a very long time.

A member of the staff walked up to Alice and introduced herself as Chloe Weston, the assistant director of hospitality. "You look lost," she said kindly.

"Overwhelmed," Alice admitted. "I arrived this afternoon and I'm not quite sure what I'm doing here."

"I see. Don't worry, we'll soon have you situated." Chloe's smile was punctuated by dimples. She wore the crisp white uniform jacket with a short black skirt and low-heeled pumps. A blond ponytail bounced up and down as she bobbed her head. "You're all checked in?"

"Yes. I'm staying in one of the condos as a guest of the owner."

"And you walked over here in this heat? Oh, my." Chloe's glance touched Alice's face, which felt damp.

She fanned herself. "I'm afraid I picked the wrong season to come to Arizona for the first time. I'm not used to the heat."

"It's terrible, I know, but never mind. There are ways to work around the temps—morning or evening activities, afternoon siestas to stay out of the monsoons and dust." Chloe's good cheer was unwavering, even when delivering that somewhat alarming spiel. "Tomorrow I'll give you a tour of the resort. We have riding stables, a huge new water park, lovely gardens, a golf course. And, of course, the spa."

She peered more closely at Alice. "Hmm. I can usually tell just by looking what type of activities a guest will prefer. But with you, I'm not sure. Are you the spa type? Hot stone, shiatsu, mud bath, herbal wrap? Let me know. Appointments have to be booked early, even in the off-season. Spa treatments are popular with our female guests."

Alice shook her head. She didn't want massages and facials, fussing and catering.

She wanted adventure.

Excitement.

Maybe romance.

Everything she'd been lacking for the past six years. No, even longer than that, if she was honest. Her life before becoming her mother's caregiver hadn't been the most eventful, either. But she'd been satisfied at the time, working as a grade-school teacher in Bangor, Maine, engaged to Stewart McKinney, a wonderful guy who'd been completely understanding when she'd had to move back to Osprey Island because of her mother's diagnosis. He'd promised to wait for Alice. They'd have the rest of their lives together.

Alice had had total faith in Stewart. Right up till the moment when the proof of his unfaithfulness had been published in the engagement announcements of the *Bangor News*.

"No spas," she said to Chloe. She glanced around the lobby, taking in the gleaming Saltillo tiles, the high beamed ceilings and the large wrought-iron chandeliers, hung three in a row to make a major statement. The guests who strolled past looked tanned, pampered and fit, despite their advanced ages. "I want to be active."

Not passive. Never again passive.

And that was *her* major statement.

"Great!" Chloe gave a quick clap. "Do you ride? Golf? I'd be happy to arrange an early-morning tee time."

"I don't golf." Alice pictured herself on the greens, a fumbling solo among the holiday-happy twosomes and foursomes. This was her opportunity to change. She'd rather not start out as a lonesome onesome. "But I'd love to try horseback riding. Not just a tame follow-the-leader trail ride, either. *Real* riding."

She could begin there and move on to more adventurous activities. Despite her major statement, even an activity as safe and easy as trail riding seemed daunting. She hadn't been on a four-legged creature since pony rides at the county fair.

"I want to gallop in the desert," she blurted. And not take a header between her mount's ears. "I want to…I want to climb and dive and race and…"

She stalled out for a moment before plunging on. "I came here to try everything."

"With that sense of adventure, you're certain to have

a super stay." Chloe gave Alice's arm a small squeeze. "Gosh, you're my favorite kind of guest. Some of them never want to get up off their biscuits. I spend my time hunting down lost sunglasses and rescheduling pool parties. I'm really going to love planning *your* days!"

Alice nodded, feeling like an impostor.

But she wasn't. She'd been wanting this for a long time. She just needed to get used to the reality of her brand-new self.

"IF YOU DON'T get out and live a little, you'll be a fuddy-duddy at forty." Leilani Blaylock Jimenez Harrison Steen powered down the computer and slid a few stray folders into a file drawer. Then she locked the drawer and dropped the key into the oversize designer handbag sitting open on one corner of the desk.

"What's a fuddy-duddy?" teased Kyle Jarreau, who sat on another corner. "Is that something the bobby-soxers used to say?"

Clearly amused, his full-figured secretary wrinkled her nose. "Pet name for my third husband."

"The one who wore tube socks to bed."

"Exactamundo." Lani gave Kyle a measuring look as she ran a comb through her short black curls polished by silver. She pulled a lipstick from her bag. "Bet you I can snare my fifth before you find a first."

"No way. Do I look like a sucker?" Kyle shifted. The closest he'd come to marriage was standing up at the recent wedding of his best friend, Gavin. The reformed bachelor had returned from his honeymoon with a deep tan and a gloating satisfaction that turned to something like pity whenever Kyle teased him about rushing home to the ball and chain.

"No," Lani said, growing thoughtful. She blotted her bright red lips on a tissue. "You look like a man so thick he doesn't even realize he's lonesome."

"Thick, huh?" Kyle patted his midsection, kept flat by rigorous workouts in the hotel's employee gym. He spent too many hours behind his desk not to adhere to a daily exercise regimen.

Lani sighed dramatically. Ever since he'd broken up his last "relationship" without turning a hair, she'd claimed he was a hopeless case. Yet she refused to give up hope. "The operative word was *lonesome*."

"I'm alone, not lonesome."

"You don't have to be either. If you'd just accept the birthday party invita—"

"I'm surrounded by people all day, every day," Kyle countered, even if that proved his thickness. He'd rather play obtuse than get into the same old debate with Lani, including her pushing him to make amends with his family. His secretary thought he needed to get a life. Kyle believed his job was his life.

Lani stood and hefted her bag by its shoulder strap. "If we're done for the day, I'm outta here, boss. Prospect Number Five is meeting me for drinks in the Manzanita Lounge." She paused in the office doorway, looking like a puffed-up pigeon teetering forward from her precarious perch on a pair of steep sandals. "You wouldn't care to join us? Sit and talk to real people face-to-face for a change? You know, the nonemployee kind?"

"No thanks," Kyle declined without regret. "You're done for the day. I'm not."

She clucked. "Ain't that the truth?" She pointed a plump finger at him. "I'm warning you—fuddy-duddy. *Before* you're forty."

He waved her away, then returned to what Lani forbiddingly termed the inner sanctum, an expansive office that was his home away from home since his promotion to resort manager. In that time he'd overseen the completion of the multimillion-dollar water park, brought in Gavin as one of his assistant managers, set up a new reservations system that would soon be implemented nationwide and seen the resort's profit margin increase substantially.

True, his personal life had suffered for all the work, including his love life. Everyone had said that Jenna, his last on-again, off-again girlfriend, was perfect for him. Everyone but the two of them, which was why ending it had been so easy.

Kyle sat behind his desk. *This* was where he belonged. The lack of personal relationships didn't bother him, despite his secretary's concern. Especially now that his extreme dedication for the past three years was about to pay off.

Big-time.

For months, the prospect of the impending performance review had been a spur in his side, propelling him forward with single-minded devotion. It was the homestretch now. He couldn't afford to slow up for a single stride.

He removed his suit jacket and cuff links. He loosened his tie. He took his cell phone out of his pants pocket and switched over to voice mail before tossing it aside. The device skidded across the surface and glanced off the single framed photograph on the desk.

Automatically, he reached out to right the photograph of his family—a group of ne'er-do-wells if ever there was one. Its presence on his desk was Lani's doing, a replacement for Jenna's head shot. Also an irritating distraction. Abruptly he thrust the photo away, facedown.

A tap of the mouse brought his computer out of sleep mode. He sat and rolled his chair closer to the desk. Time for serious work.

After forty-five minutes studying the monthly reports from his department managers, Kyle stopped to straighten and stretch. He relished these early-evening hours, with his staff gone home and the Prince Montez East Coast management offices shut down. As long as there were no emergency calls from the evening concierge, he could get a lot of work accomplished. Normally he dove into it with gusto, putting in another two hours before his empty stomach forced him into calling room service.

But not this evening. Lani's words nagged at him.

Fuddy-duddy. *Lonesome.*

Kyle stood and moved restlessly around the sparsely furnished space before pausing at one of the three tall windows that overlooked the stone courtyard and Moorish fountain at the center of the resort complex. Towering palms lined the long curve of the main road, as well as the various paths leading away from it. In the distance, beyond the foothills, was the humpbacked crest of Camelback Mountain, cast blood orange in the fading sun.

He was unaccountably distracted by the vista. When was the last time he'd noticed a sunset?

He turned suddenly and grabbed the picture off his desk, relocating it to one of the nearly empty shelves in the storage unit along one of the unadorned walls.

Kyle didn't bother much with the trappings of his position—an expense account, a company car and driver, the large office for work and the luxury suite for sleep. They were valuable only for the air of success they gave him. That, admittedly, he savored.

From the shelf, the faces of his family mocked him. *Think you're a big shot?*

"Hell, yeah," he said softly.

What about us? Didja forget us?

He swung away. Hadn't he done enough for them? Late-night calls to lawyers, arguments mediated, loans that would never be repaid. Strings pulled, jobs acquired, christenings and bail hearings and holidays attended, each one invariably ending in an argument.

Lani was wrong. He'd put in plenty of face-to-face time. Real people were highly overrated.

There was a staccato rap on the door. Gavin Brill thrust his head inside. "Hey, Jarreau. I'm on my way home."

"Give my best to the wife." Kyle's gut seized. He must be hungry.

"Sorry, man." Gavin raised his eyebrows. At a scarce five-six, he was eight inches shorter than Kyle, but considered handsome by the women around the office. They swooned over his jet-black hair, blue eyes and Hollywood profile. "I'll be too busy giving her mine."

"No one likes a braggart."

Gavin grinned. "I can't help it."

Kyle scowled; this was their act. "How many times did you call her today?"

Gavin had married Melina, one of their former reservation clerks. A cute little brunette who thought he was the sun and the moon and all the stars, too. Her adoration seemed cloying to Kyle, but he gave the couple allowances to be sappy newlyweds. Not that he'd admit it to Gavin.

The man's grin widened. "Only eight. You owe me twenty."

"Yeah, but how many times did *she* call you?"

"That wasn't part of the bet."

"A technicality," Kyle said, but he took out his wallet. "I only have a hundred."

Gavin gestured with his head. "Walk down with me and we'll change it at the front desk."

"You know I'm good for the money."

"C'mon, bud. Don't be a stick in the mud."

First a fuddy-duddy and now a stick in the mud?

"I can offer extra incentive," Gavin said. "Your unexpected arrival will put the fear of authority in the new night concierge. I hear he's been hell on the staff, trying to prove himself."

"Sounds like he has the right idea."

To demonstrate that he wasn't a fuddy, let alone a duddy, Kyle didn't bother to roll down his sleeves and put on his jacket. They walked past the elevator to the stairwell and jogged down four flights, neither willing to break the pace.

"Melina says…" Gavin pushed through the staff door that opened onto a hidden corner of the vast lobby. He'd missed more than a few of their workouts lately and was trying not to pant. "Her friends at the desk—"

"Not my concern," Kyle interrupted so the guy could inhale. Unless the minor problem had potential to grow into a larger issue, he'd learned to let his department managers deal with petty staff complaints. "Remember the chain of command."

Gavin slid a finger inside his collar. "That's what I told Melina you'd say, but she…" He shrugged. "She thought you'd care."

"Care?" The word came out more sharply than Kyle had intended. He didn't think of himself as uncaring, even when it came to his family. Just strict. With the Jarreaus, fed up.

"I meant, if I brought up the problem on her friends' behalf," Gavin explained. "She doesn't get that you don't play favorites on the job."

"The new concierge is only establishing the proper authority over his staff," Kyle said, but he was uneasy. He *had* played favorites. Hiring both his foolish sister and his scoundrel younger brother was nepotism at its finest. The family ties he hadn't been able to completely break.

Except for that small show of weakness, he'd been relentless in his climb up the corporate ladder. He was weeks away from a promotion that was a rare achievement for a man of thirty-six. Why should he have misgivings now?

Because he'd rather be respected by his staff than beloved?

Or was it because Lani had called him lonesome?

Or because Gavin had both a successful career and an adoring wife?

Kyle scanned the luxurious lobby. A reassuring sight. The lights of the stately yet rustic chandeliers cast a glow over ocher stucco walls. Tall palm fronds softened the empty corners. Guests moved about leisurely, most of them on their way to one of the lounges or restaurants. The bustle of white-jacketed employees was constant but discreet, as was the subtle infusion of music from a harpist and piano player on one of the overhanging balconies.

Only one woman seemed out of place—a rather plain brunette, unobtrusive except for a brightly colored outfit that shouted its newness. She was noticeable because she stood alone at the entrance, rubbing her hands on her skirt while she gawked at the teak front desk and the potted orange trees and the skylights that opened the lobby to the lavender-tinged sky.

An employee from the hospitality staff gestured to the solitary woman. They walked to the restaurant entrance, holding an animated conversation as if they were old friends.

Satisfied that his employee was doing her job, Kyle erased the new guest from his mind and went to make change at the desk. He wished that all the day's distractions were as easily forgotten.

CHAPTER TWO

"IS IT JUST my imagination, or is almost everyone here kind of old?" Alice asked as she and Chloe walked toward the entrance of the restaurant. The hospitality director had explained that while there were several fine dining spots at the resort, the Oasis de la Luna was the best.

"The guests, that is," Alice corrected herself. "Not the staff."

Chloe chuckled. "I suppose you're right. We do cater to an upscale older crowd. Not quite as much during the off-season, however. This is discount time, when we get more families on tight budgets. But there are always plenty of retirees who stick around, too."

"Especially at the condos." Alice hesitated. "I noticed when I arrived that the other residents were mostly senior citizens. I'm not saying there's anything wrong with that. I was just hoping for a diverse crowd." Pah! She was hoping for young single men.

"Of course you're right," Chloe said breezily. "A number of the condos are owned by year-round senior residents. The snowbirds with two homes are the ones who move down in the winter and fly back north for the summer."

"They seemed friendly." Except for one old lady

who'd been scooting along the sidewalk on a Segway. She'd almost run Alice over.

"Very friendly, some of them. Watch out or they'll adopt you."

Alice nodded. While following a porter through the Spanish-style condominium village when she'd first arrived, she'd been waved at and helloed to by the poolside loungers. They'd called her over to join them, but she'd only waved back. After her long trip, she'd been eager to get out of the stifling heat and unpack.

"Thanks for the warning," she said. "I don't want to spend my entire vacation playing canasta and taking naps." She'd had enough experience with that pace of life to keep her until she was eighty.

"The condo gangs seem to be into poker these days. And you might be surprised. Some of them are quite lively."

"Oh, I'm sure they are. I didn't mean to stereotype, it's just that…" Alice broke off; she didn't want to delve too deeply into her close acquaintance with the gray-haired set on Osprey Island. "I was hoping for more action. My mother and her friends, um…"

They had reached the entrance and were waiting for the maître d' to return. Chloe looked at Alice. "Yes?"

Emotion had clotted in her throat. "You see, I was caring for my sick mother for a long time, and my life got to revolve around hers. Four months ago, she passed on. So, basically, I'm at loose ends. This trip is a new start for me."

Chloe was sympathetic. "I hear you. You're turning a fresh page. You want something different. *Not* the over-sixties crowd from the condos."

"Yes," Alice said gratefully.

"No problem! I'll see to it that you have an especially exciting stay." The dimples reappeared in Chloe's small round face, one high on her cheek, two others framing her rosebud mouth. "I've got all sorts of ideas for activities galore."

"Keep them within reason." Alice couldn't prevent a note of caution from creeping into her voice. "I talk a good game, but I'm not sure how daring I'll actually be."

"Naturally, the safety and comfort of our guests are our primary concerns," Chloe said, but then she added, almost to herself, "Hmm, what about Camelback? And rock climbing…"

Oh, dear. "Right now, I'd settle for dinner. It's been a long day."

"Of course." Chloe waved impatiently for the maître d' while surveying the busy dining room. "I'll get you a good table. Would you prefer the patio?"

"Anything will do," Alice said. The clink of silverware, the murmur of conversation and soft harp music were inviting. She watched a handsome, suntanned couple lean close over the flicker of a tea light and wished she wasn't alone.

Never mind. Make the best of it.

"Even by the kitchen," she added.

"*Pfft.* You deserve better than that."

I do, Alice silently agreed. She'd spoken out of habit. Like most Osprey Islanders, she was accustomed to humility. Ostentation was not appreciated there.

While Chloe conferred with the maître d', Alice gazed at the elegant dining room. The rustic stone, wood and stucco of the lobby gave way to a more refined Spanish design with arches, glass lanterns and wrought-iron sconces. White linen and exotic birds of paradise dressed the tables.

Alice smoothed her skirt. It was a style she'd never worn before, striped like a flag in fiesta colors that suddenly seemed too garish and common. When she'd bought it, she'd imagined herself sipping sangria under an umbrella on a sunny patio, not sticking out like a cheap piñata at an exquisite soirée.

"All righty," Chloe said. "You've got a table by the window, but it won't be ready for another ten or fifteen minutes. I'd love to take you for a drink in the Manzanita Lounge. It's right through here."

"You don't have to stick with me." Alice lowered her eyes so that the other woman wouldn't see how much she really didn't want to be on her own tonight. "I'm sure you have other guests to attend to."

"I can spare ten minutes." Chloe looped a hand around Alice's elbow. "In fact, you'd be doing me a favor. The new night concierge is a taskmaster. I don't get to mingle with guests very often since he came on the job."

"Well, if you put it that way…" Alice said with a light laugh that eased the strain in her throat. She wasn't as prepared for this adventure as she'd have liked.

Tomorrow, she told herself. Tomorrow she'd have adjusted and would feel more equipped.

They went into the adjacent lounge and sat at the bar to order drinks. The bartender was a good-looking young Mexican whose dark eyes were set off by the high collar of the staff uniform. After serving them with a flourish, he was called away to the other end of the bar.

"Do you know him?" Alice whispered before taking a sip of a prickly-pear-flavored rum punch.

Chloe had settled for the nonalcoholic version. "Ramon? He's new. Cute, don't you think?"

"Young."

"He's putting himself through college, but he started late. He's only a year younger than I am."

"You're young, too." This was one of the times that thirty-four and never a bride seemed ancient to Alice. "Sounds like you know him pretty well."

"We've talked." Chloe grinned. "And flirted." She swiveled to gaze longingly down the polished stone bar before swinging her stool back in Alice's direction. "What about you? No significant other waiting for you at home?"

Alice spun her straw, swirling the ice in her drink. "No one."

Chloe's eyes creased. They were tilted up at the corners by the pull of her tightly anchored high ponytail. "Has your heart been broken?"

Alice blinked. Did it still show? She'd been jilted by Stewart almost five years ago.

Five years—wow. She hadn't added it up lately. She felt as if the breakup had only recently happened. Yet she knew that she'd been lucky to be rid of the faithless man and that there were much deeper losses.

Under normal circumstances, she might have been able to get over Stewart and move on. But romantic options on Osprey were limited. She'd been left with far too many empty hours to brood.

"Water under the bridge," she said, putting on a nonchalant front. "And way down the river."

Chloe nodded sagely. "We've all watched that stream flow by."

"Some of us more than others," said a plump, older woman who was passing by. "My rowboat's capsized a few times, but I keep on paddling." She raised her hand, calling out, "Yoo-hoo, cutie!" to a silver-haired man in cowboy boots and a bolo tie before hurrying away.

"That's Leilani Steen," Chloe said, "assistant to the boss."

"The taskmaster?" Alice asked.

"Not *my* taskmaster. A different one. Actually quite a hot one, if he'd ever loosen his tie and pop off his cuff links." Chloe spun right around, sitting straighter as she did. "Speak of the devil. There he is now."

Alice glanced over her shoulder and saw the rowboat woman talking to someone who towered over her, while the woman's suitor hovered at her elbow. "Which taskmaster?"

"Lani's boss. Mr. Kyle Jarreau." Chloe's tone was filled with admiration. "Manager of the whole PM shebang."

PM meant Prince Montez, Alice remembered, as a second look had her straightening up right alongside Chloe. There was something about the man who'd just walked into the lounge that made a woman draw a breath all the way to the bottom of her lungs.

Lani and her date had moved on and the "taskmaster" stood alone in the archway between bar and restaurant. Alone but at ease, his presence effortlessly commanding as he surveyed the area.

The air in the room became electric, the employees galvanized. Alice rubbed her palms over the goose bumps on her arms. She swiveled toward the bar. The back of her head and neck tingled as if he'd looked her way.

"Uh-oh," Chloe said without moving her lips. "He's seen me."

Alice exhaled. *Not me. Of course, not me.* "You'd better go on, then. I don't want to keep you from your job."

Chloe slid off the stool. "Have a nice dinner." She laid her hand on Alice's arm. "I'll be in touch tomorrow and we'll plan your schedule."

Alice watched obliquely as Chloe passed the boss with a nodding bounce of her ponytail and a perky, "Good evening, Mr. Jarreau."

He returned the nod without smiling.

He was solemn, but young for such a position of authority. Probably no more than forty, tops. Not that Alice knew much about the ins and outs of resort management, her only experience being the cakes she'd delivered to the White Gull Inn from her best friend Susan's bakery.

She tipped forward and caught the straw between her teeth. The tingles returned, but when she flicked her gaze at Mr. Jarreau, he wasn't looking her way. She wished he'd move. Go away. Prove that there was no cat-and-mouse awareness except in her overheated imagination.

Suddenly he appeared beside her, leaning past Chloe's abandoned stool with his hands on the edge of the granite slab of the bar. He pressed forward, flexing tanned forearms beneath the rolled-up sleeves of his shirt. "Busy night, Ramon?"

Loose tie, no cuff links, Alice noted with a shiver. Only a chunky platinum watch around one thick wrist. Chloe had got it wrong.

The bartender smiled, revealing his white teeth. "The usual, sir. The conference attendees drained five gallons of margarita mix in twenty minutes flat. Chef Chavez is causing a ruckus in the kitchens. Can I get you anything, Mr. Jarreau?"

"No." He pushed away from the bar, ran his dangling

tie between two fingers. "Yes. I'll have a whiskey sour. Light on the whiskey. I have an empty stomach."

While Ramon busied himself, Jarreau's glance rested on Alice for a second. She felt overly conscious of her elbows pressed to her ribs and her tongue against her teeth.

I'm nothing to him. Just another guest. One face among hundreds.

The thought rankled her. Why was she so dismissive of herself? Had her status as everybody's helpmate become that ingrained?

"It's a beautiful hotel," she said. Her voice seemed too eager, too bright, if only to herself. "That is, from what I've seen so far. I just arrived a few hours ago. Chloe Weston was showing me around." *Now I'm talking too much.* "She was very kind and welcoming. A real credit to the resort."

"Excellent." Mr. Jarreau took his drink from the bartender, and Alice didn't know which of them he was addressing until he raised his glass to her. "Enjoy your stay."

"Thanks." Deep breath. "I'm Alice Potter. From Osprey Island, Maine."

"Kyle Jarreau. Pleased to meet you."

There was a moment of awkward silence. She felt compelled to fill it. "I know what you're thinking." She was plucking words from the whirl of her brain. "Alice Potter is such a nursery rhyme kind of name."

"Huh," he said, half a chuckle.

The maître d' had appeared at her other elbow. "Your table is ready, Miss Potter."

She shot an amused glance at Mr. Jarreau as she disembarked. "You see what I mean?"

His mouth moved without quite reaching a smile. "Good evening." One eyebrow tilted. "Miss Potter."

Alice laughed and walked away. The swish of her full skirt no longer felt gaudy. It was festive.

KYLE STAYED at the bar in the Manzanita Lounge, ordering a turkey club sandwich from the grill. He chatted with Ramon about hoops and colleges and then college hoops during the bartender's few quiet moments. That'd show Lani, he thought to himself at one point, even though the gibe felt immature when she was only thinking of his goodwill. His own mother had never been the type to monitor his social progress. She'd rarely even remembered to tell him to eat his vegetables.

From his position, he could see into the neighboring restaurant. At a distant table, a small one tucked in a corner beside a window, sat Miss Potter. Solo. His eyes returned to her again and again throughout the hour, watching as she alternately stared dreamily out the window and scribbled in a small notebook she set aside only when her dinner was served.

Alice Potter of Osprey Island, Maine. She was nothing extraordinary. Mild, affable, a little awkward. And yet something about her had engaged his interest.

Her gentle brown eyes…her tremulous attempt at witty conversation?

He considered, watching a smile light her face when a waiter arrived with her dessert, a miniature tower of cake drizzled with fruit and chocolate sauce. She studied the plate for a moment, then picked up a fork, pausing only to look around the room with an expectant smile that went unreturned. Her pleasure dimmed as she focused on the dessert.

Kyle gritted his teeth. Perhaps it was her loneliness that drew him.

He glanced away, fully aware that his continuing presence had put the lounge employees on edge. They hurried back and forth, giving their patrons one level above the usual top-notch service. None had taken a break to dally at the bar and shoot the breeze with Ramon the way they usually might.

They would be dying for Kyle to leave already. Not a single one of them would believe that the pressure on him to deliver far outweighed theirs. Some days—and some solitary middle-of-the-nights—he felt as though an elephant sat on his chest.

He lifted a finger to the bartender, who reacted instantly. The attentiveness meant everything to Kyle. He had command. He'd instilled in the staff a discipline that matched his own. Those things were more important than fleeting gratification or needy personal relationships that only caused trouble.

Ramon parked his fists on his hips. "Can I get you another, boss?"

The plate from Kyle's meal had been removed, but a small pool of alcohol remained in his glass. "No, thanks. One's my limit." He crooked a finger. "Tell me…"

The bartender leaned in.

"When I leave, will the entire staff go on break at once?"

After a startled moment, Ramon smiled. "They'll wait five minutes to be sure you're gone."

Kyle nodded. "That's what I thought." He pushed aside a crumpled cocktail napkin, dropped his feet to the floor. "Prepare for the mass exodus."

He stood and turned, catching sight of Alice Potter

again. A waiter was taking away her dessert plate. She glanced at the other diners, catching her bottom lip with her teeth.

"I changed my mind," he said to the young bartender. "Give me two glasses of champagne, please."

"Right away."

Kyle saw that all charges were added to his account, along with a hefty tip for Ramon, then carried the fine crystal into the restaurant. It had begun to empty out, but a number of patrons lingered over drinks to enjoy the Old World atmosphere.

Alice Potter was leaning forward on stiff arms as she gazed out the window at the twinkle of the patio lights and the dark sky beyond. She looked up with surprise when Kyle set the champagne flute in front of her.

"Miss Potter," he said. "Your first night here deserves to be toasted with champagne. May I join you?"

Her fingers fluttered to her hair, worn shoulder-length in a rather shapeless brown bob. "Of course. But could we go outside to the patio? I was just thinking that I'd like to sit under the stars."

He picked up the flutes. "Lead the way."

She rose, hesitant as she reached for her handbag. "I haven't paid the—"

"It's taken care of."

"Oh. Thank you. Thank you so much." She seemed uncertain about accepting. "I suppose you can do that, charge it to the house, when you *are* the house."

"Yes," he said slowly. So she knew who he was. "Although I'm not really the house. Merely the overseer." He caught the handle of the patio door with two fingers just as she reached for it, too. Their finger-tips pressed.

She yanked her hand away. A waiter stepped in, holding the door open and smoothly relieving Kyle of the glasses.

There was an open table at the periphery, where sage and lavender swayed in the breeze. Kyle held out a chair for Alice.

She glanced at him with a shy smile as he seated himself. "You're so mannerly."

"I learned to be," he admitted. "That's not how I grew up."

"Oh?"

He shrugged off her questioning look, not willing to go there. "You're a long way from home."

She sipped her champagne, quite the lady herself. "That's the idea." She turned her head toward the cooling breeze rolling in off the mountains. "I wanted to be as far away as I could manage. In an unfamiliar place."

"You've never been to the Southwest before?"

"Not since a high-school class trip to Mazatlán. I haven't been very adventurous. But I'm going to make up for that." She made a face, and he liked her wry honesty, even the humility.

"During dinner," she continued, "I was working on a list."

His interest deepened. "May I see it?"

"Oh, no, it's embarrassing."

"Come on," he coaxed.

Her cheeks were pink, her eyes large and velvety dark, dominating her oval face. She was almost pretty. "It's nothing. Only a standard list of things to do and places to go while I'm here."

"Then it can't be embarrassing."

"That depends. You don't think it's embarrassing for

a thirty-four-year-old woman to admit that she has about as much experience as a potted plant?"

Kyle grinned. "I doubt that's true."

She returned the grin, erasing every trace of exhaustion and sadness from her expression. "Nearly."

He wanted to touch her. Instead, he put his elbows on the table and folded his hands against his chin, holding her gaze while he dug a thumbnail into his bottom lip. "Read me something off the list."

After a moment, she looked away, blushing even more. "I'll find an innocuous item." She pulled the pocket notebook from her bag and flipped the pages where her scrawled handwriting looped.

She saw him peeking and shielded the list from view. She cleared her throat. "Here's one—see a rattlesnake."

He raised his eyebrows. "At least you don't want to pet it."

"It's silly, I know. But I've never seen a rattlesnake. We don't have them in Maine."

"What else is on the list?"

"Get a picture taken with a saguaro cactus," she read. "That's not very exciting, is it?"

"Don't pet the cactus, either."

She rolled her eyes, but her shoulders relaxed and she took another drink of champagne. Pages turned. "Hmm." Her smile was almost flirtatious. "I can cross off *this* one." She searched in her purse for a pen.

"What is it?"

She clicked the pen. "Drinks on the patio with a handsome stranger."

"You're making that up."

"No, really. See?" She held up the book, showing him the line she'd drawn through number fourteen.

"I was number fourteen?"

"Well after the rattlesnake." Her eyes met his. "I was working up to the really good ones."

Warmth seeped into his face. He was glad he'd already loosened his tie. "What's number fifteen? Maybe we can knock that one off, too."

She turned the page. "Meet a cowboy."

Kyle frowned. "Your fantasies aren't very evolved."

"That kinda feels like an insult, but I know what you mean." She laughed. "I suppose I'm a slow starter. Except, well, they're not fantasies, are they? Fantasies are…"

"Kiss a cowboy?" he suggested, knowing he shouldn't. Her face turned even redder and she thrust the notebook back into her purse. He'd thought a drink with Alice Potter would be harmless, a mild conversation about resort amenities and the weather forecast. He'd thought he was doing it to make *her* feel better.

Not to make himself feel human.

Human? Try feeling like a *man*.

She was not a stunner, not sophisticated or smooth. Nothing like Jenna. But she was clever and gentle. She brought out his protective instincts.

"Why did you come here?" he asked. "This resort, specifically."

She was concentrating on her champagne, taking tiny sip after tiny sip. "Is this a customer survey?"

"Curiosity. You're different from our usual guest."

Her head came up. "Meaning I'm not seventy years old and wealthy?"

"And you're…single. We're not known as a singles resort, even though I've tried to expand our market." He was striving to sound professional, which had never been a problem before.

"It's not a spectacular story," Alice said. "I just needed to get away from home. One day I was surfing the Internet, looking for interesting places I'd never been to, when I landed on a site that specializes in vacation-home exchanges. Long story short, I swapped two weeks with a condo owner. He's staying at my cottage in Maine." She toyed with the stem of her glass, her head bent to one side so her neck was exposed.

Kyle's eyes lingered. "I see. So you're in one of the condos." Master of stating the obvious.

No wonder she'd made the seventy-year-old comment. The Prince Montez chain had plunged into the thriving vacation-condo market as an adjunct to their luxury resort hotels. While the condos were technically under Kyle's command, that wasn't an area where he needed to spend a lot of his time. Other than the occasional turnover of ownership or HOA—Home Owner's Association—tussle, their management was a matter of maintaining the status quo.

"I don't get over to the condos very often," he said.

That meant he wasn't likely to come across Alice after tonight. Probably a good thing. One "welcome" drink was fine, but he couldn't afford to give her the idea that he was interested in her. The PM policy against fraternization between guests and employees was strictly enforced—by him. Although romantic relationships among employees was also frowned on, they happened more frequently than he would have preferred. Take Gavin, for example.

"I'm kept busy here," he added, not sure why he felt the need to explain himself to Alice, except that she looked almost forlorn. A fringe of overly long bangs had fallen across her forehead, into her eyes.

"Yes." She studied her fingers, caged around the glass.

Kyle clenched his jaw. He had fired two employees for fraternization. One a guy who'd played cabana boy a little too well, following up on the offers of flirtatious female guests, even after several warnings. The other had been an office worker, though fraternization had been the least of her crimes. She'd also been more than an employee to Kyle. His sister, in fact. Making her flouting of the rules a most uncomfortable situation.

But he'd done what he had to do. And he would do it again, even if that meant letting down sweet Alice Potter with her nursery rhyme name and her large dark eyes that held so much expectation and hope.

His fault, damn it. She'd have had no hopes if he hadn't already stepped over the line.

"Thank you for sharing my company," he said, rising to his feet. *For making me number fourteen.* "I enjoyed it."

She looked up at him, blinking, then brushed her hair aside. "I did, too," she said softly.

"Please let…let the staff know if you need anything at all during your stay with us."

"Yes, thank you."

"Would you like an escort back to the condo? We have carts available, or—"

"No, thank you. Now that it's cooled off, I'll enjoy the walk. The grounds are so beautiful." She turned her face away, lifting it again to the balmy breeze. His gaze followed hers across the manicured vista, where guests strolled by twos and threes. Farther off, snatches of music played intermittently as the more garrulous groups entered the adjacent nightclub. "I'd like to stay here for a while longer."

Kyle hesitated, but there seemed nothing left to say.

He could *not* ask her to go dancing. "Good evening, then, Miss Potter."

Her lips parted. "Good evening, Mr. Jarreau." She did not meet his eyes.

THE LONESOME ONESOME, Alice thought with derision as she accepted a second glass of champagne from the attentive waiter, even though one was enough to make her tipsy.

She supposed she qualified as a VIP now that she'd been noticed by the head honcho, but she couldn't enjoy the moment of glory, such as it was. She'd rather have stayed anonymous than be given a taste of what it felt like to be admired and even flirted with before the attention was taken away again.

But that was the old Alice talking.

The new Alice should have been bolder. Made herself too enticing to resist. Somehow.

Her interlude with Kyle Jarreau was likely the only holiday flirtation she'd get. She would savor it when she was home.

Home alone.

No, focus on Kyle. The way he held himself, for instance—erect and almost regal, evoking formality even with his button-down shirt undone at the cuffs and collar. His posture was so perfect that she'd reminded herself several times to sit up, lift her head high to meet his gaze.

His hair, for another. Short and thick, deep walnut brown and tipped with the slightest touch of honey. His eyes had been almost the same shade. Serious eyes, even when he'd teased her about the list.

She closed her own eyes now, remembering his strong hands, the quick grin, the hint of stubble on his firm jaw, the masculine fuzz on his tanned forearms.

The moment at the door when their fingers had touched.

She'd felt a blazingly intense awareness—of his skin, the heat of him, the solid muscle and discipline and careful control.

Alice pressed her fingertips together hard enough to hurt. She released them and let her hands fall to her lap, curled like limp macaroni as she looked up at the stars and sighed. No sense wishing on *them* anymore. She'd asked for a handsome stranger and she'd been given one.

Oh, yes. Kyle Jarreau had fulfilled the requirements very well.

Perhaps too well, considering that, despite their apparent connection, he'd seemed determined to remain a stranger.

Prince Montez Oasis Resort, Phoenix, Arizona— the jewel of the Sonoran desert.

July 21
Dear Mom,
I'm not going to actually mail this postcard, but it makes a funny kind of sense that the first one I write should be to you. You're the one who encouraged me to take this trip, in so many more ways than just $$. So I'm here, and I'm going to do you proud. I've already begun—and how!— but I'll send *that* postcard to Sue. I'm writing to you, Mom, to say thanks for the inspiration.
Love,
Alice

CHAPTER THREE

ALICE AWOKE EARLY the next morning and got into the shower, emerging revived and ready to take on every activity the resort offered. The list she'd written had proved how much of her life she'd let slip away the past six years on Osprey Island.

She would never, absolutely never, regret being there for her mother as the initial occurrence of breast cancer had returned, then spread. Family was family. But Alice also recognized that the cost to herself had been high. At a time when many others her age were settled with jobs, marriage, kids, she had nothing but a one-half share in a run-down little cottage and a spotty job history of temporary positions. Nursemaid, gardener, part-time baker, fill-in babysitter, substitute teacher.

She had a substitute life.

But no more! Alice brushed her teeth and pulled a comb through her wet hair, wrinkling her nose at the mirror. She'd made promises to herself.

She dropped her damp towel and got into the thick terry robe with the PM crest on the lapel. It was good to feel pampered.

She strolled into the living room, captivated anew by the exotic surroundings. Last night, she'd pulled the louvered wood shutters across the windows and sliding glass doors. Now the early-morning sunshine had reached past the dusty red foothills that bordered the resort complex to stripe the floor with light. She curled her bare toes into the heat. All around her was adobe and slate, brushed steel, ebony wood and Sinatra-era furnishings with low, straight lines. So different from the dumpy, flowery pieces and peeling paint at the cottage back home.

Everything's different now. I'm a woman on the verge of a whole new life.

The doorbell chimed.

"Cripes," she said, touching her hair, pulling at the neckline of the robe. She didn't know anyone here, except...

Maybe it was Chloe.

The bell chimed again, and she hurried to open the door.

"Welcome to Wrinkle Resort!" Five seniors—three women and two men—crowded close, each as tanned as Kraft paper.

"She's a youngster," said a large, sharp-eyed man. He wore a black toupee above thick gray sideburns and matching gnarly eyebrows.

"Myrna saw you arrive," announced one of the women as she pushed herself into the room. The others followed when Alice politely stepped aside. "And so did the Pool Sharks."

"But we were taking our siestas."

"Late afternoon, until the sun drops."

"Most everyone does."

"Except the Pool Sharks, led by Arthur Banyon. He's a lizard. He basks in the sun."

The man in a Panama hat snorted. "Sure, but he's seventy and he'd pass for a hundred."

"She doesn't care about Arthur," said a second

woman, who was small but forceful, in a T-shirt that advertised Cuervo Gold.

Alice was amused. The older women on Osprey Island didn't wear tequila shirts. Maybe Joe D's Crab Shack, if they were characters.

The woman eyed Alice blatantly. "Where ya from, honey?"

She clutched the lapel of the white robe. "Maine."

"Maine!" The answer set off a buzz. "All that way."

"Are you related to the Raffertys?" one of them asked. "What happened to the Raffertys?"

The first man gestured for silence. "Introductions first." He pumped Alice's hand. "This gang here is known as the Cocktail Shakers, rivals to the Sharks. I'm Walter St. Gregory. This is my wife, Mags." The woman with the Lucille Ball curls. "Forgive us for barging in so early. We should have waited, but the gals were impatient."

Mags nodded. "We were expecting the Raffertys."

"Sorry. It's just me." Through the Holidays Away agency, Alice had swapped vacation homes with a man named Sean Rafferty, who was a state trooper from Massachusetts. He'd written in one of his e-mails that the condo belonged to his retired parents, who used it for vacations. "I don't actually know the Raffertys. I'm staying here on a house swap."

The group was taken aback. "A swap! My goodness," Mags said.

"I've heard of them," said the woman in the tequila shirt. She pursed her lips, which made her narrow face look even narrower. "Then where are the Raffertys?"

"At my house. On Osprey Island. But it's not the Raffertys, it's only their son."

"That doesn't sound like the Raffertys. They always have their grandson from California come to visit while he's on summer vacation. What did you say your name was?"

"Alice Potter. The, um, Prince Montez management is fully informed. I have the keys and a letter of agreement."

The third woman patted Alice's arm. "I'm Mary Grace Malone. Alice is such a sweet, old-fashioned name and I can see it fits you. Don't mind Harrie. She was a private investigator for thirty-eight years. Nothing happens in the resort without her getting the details."

Harrie winked. "Harriet Humbert, at your service. If you need a clue."

Alice laughed. "I…well, I probably do."

"You'll learn your way around soon enough," she sympathized.

"What did you call this place?" Alice asked. "Some nickname?"

"Wrinkle Resort," said Walter, spreading expansive hands to encompass his elderly cohorts. "You can see why."

Alice gulped. The median age was as she'd suspected. "Are there any younger people around?"

"Sure, up at the hotel," Harrie said. She wiggled her narrow hips. "Every night, at the club and the bars."

Walter scowled. "We get a bunch of families, too, especially with the new water park. Hellions, most of 'em. Between them and the Pool Sharks, you'll want to avoid the pools in the peak hours."

"Oh," Alice said.

"Look at her." Mags pinched Alice's cheek. "Don't worry, sweetheart. There's plenty going on for the young singles, too. Anytime you want, get yourself all gussied up and Wally will drive you up to the disco in his golf cart."

Alice imagined making an entrance on the arm of the large and blustery Walter. "We'll have to do that one of these nights." She smiled and crossed her fingers inside the robe's deep pockets. "But for now, I've got a busy day planned." Potentially.

"Then we'll leave you to get dressed." Mary Grace moved toward the door. The others reluctantly followed.

"Just remember," Walter said, "you're welcome to join the Cocktail Shakers anytime."

"We're the fun bunch," Harrie put in. "Always a good time."

"Tonight's Margarita Madness," crowed the Panama hat man, using a bad Latin accent. "Five o'clock, under the umbrellas by the pool. We're clearing out the Sharks if we have to attack with water guns."

Walter backed out, hands cupped around an invisible martini shaker at shoulder level. He gave it a vigorous shake. "We do a different cocktail every evening. You'd be a fine addition to our merry band, Miss Potter."

Alice nodded. "Thanks, Mr. St. Gregory. I appreciate the invitation. I promise to stop by eventually. I'm here for two weeks."

"Call us Wally and Mags."

"Reg and M.G.," called Panama hat from the breezeway, his arm around Mary Grace.

"And don't forget Harrie!"

"As if I could." Alice laughed and waved and shut the door. She stared wide-eyed at the empty room before letting out her breath.

Okay, so maybe there wouldn't be a lot of glamour

and adventure to her vacation. Maybe, even after all her resolutions, she'd end up doing crossword puzzles and drinking strange cocktails by the pool. She was still determined to enjoy herself.

Don't surrender yet. According to the brochures, the resort offered horseback riding, off-road biking and hiking, desert-jeep tours. Even skydiving.

Staying on the ground seemed like a good idea for now. She'd already made one big leap of faith.

"HOWDY, THERE, ma'am. Now ain't yew a fine filly?" The stablehand pushed a battered straw Stetson to the back of his head. "Y'lookin' for a bronc?"

Number fifteen. Alice ran her palms down her jeans before extending a hand. *Meet a cowboy.* At this rate, she'd have to come up with a new list before the first week was out.

"I'm Alice Potter. Chloe sent me."

"You mean that sweet li'l gal with the blond pony-tail?" Plastering a wide grin across his tanned face, the man shook her hand. He was straight from central casting: handsome weathered face, golden-brown lock tumbled across his forehead, clear green eyes, shoulders as broad as his cowpoke accent. A white tank and low-riding jeans clung to his lean hard body. His boots were pointy-toed and emerald green. Bought to match his eyes, she'd just bet.

Alice nodded. "Chloe said you would set me up with a lesson or two. I've already signed on for a trail ride, but I'd like to learn a few techniques first so I know what I'm doing. I'm a beginner."

The cowboy slid an arm around her shoulders and gave her an encouraging hug. "Don'tcha worry none, li'l lady. I'll have you gallopin' 'cross the desert in two shakes of a rattler's tail."

That startled her—how did he know she dreamed of galloping across the desert? Did everyone have the same secret desire? She tried to squirm away. The cowboy smelled of leather, cologne and pungent sweat. The proximity of so much male made her stomach swirl. She stepped out from under his arm and looked into a stall, pretending an interest in the four-legged occupant. The stable was quiet and dark. At the other end of the building, a lone female stablehand shoveled out one of the stalls, pitching forkfuls into a wheelbarrow.

"That there bay's name is Loco," said the cowboy. "Y'think you'd like to climb aboard?"

An extremely large brown horse stuck its black nose against the upper rails of the stall, nostrils flaring as he snorted the way Alice imagined a charging bull might. "Heck, no."

The cowboy slid open the stall door. The horse swung around to greet him, its long black tail swishing across its hocks. "Pay the name no mind, ma'am. This old fella's gentle as a lamb."

She stayed far back as he led the horse out into the aisle. "What about you? Have you got a name?"

"Y'can call me Denver," he said, nodding and grinning. His eyes swept her up and down with obvious approval. "If I can call yew Allie."

Denver the cowboy. Perfect.

A little too perfect. Especially the lingo. She supposed he'd been hired to give the guests a show.

"My name's Alice," she said, thinking he'd misheard.

"Maybe so, but yew look like an Allie. Y'know—all cute 'n sassy."

"Me?" Her hair was caught up in a clip and she'd knotted her sleeveless checked blouse at the waist. Did that qualify as sassy? Or was her new attitude showing already?

After the Cocktail Shakers had gone, Chloe had phoned with suggestions for the day—a riding lesson this morning and a trip to the wave pool in the afternoon. What she'd called an easy start had seemed plenty adventurous to Alice, particularly now that she was face-to-face with a cowboy and a horse. She wasn't afraid of horses. Or cowboys. She just had a healthy caution about riding—or kissing—either one.

That darn Kyle Jarreau. *He'd* put the notion in her head.

Denver hooked a rope to the horse's halter and handed the end of it to Alice. "By gosh, you're cute as a pigtailed pup when you're blushin'."

He flirts with every woman. Alice was certain of that, but she was flattered all the same. Back home on the island, she knew everyone as well as they knew her. Flirting with Keith at the inn or Bill the kayak guy would be like flirting with a cousin.

Standing at the end of the horse's lead, she looked sidelong at Denver. Her lips curved invitingly. "I'll bet you make all the women blush."

With an unabashed wink that did nothing to deny her claim, he tossed a saddle blanket over the horse's back. His lashes were as thick as a girl's.

So were the horse's, fringing large brown eyes that watched her with interest. Alice swallowed and stepped closer to the animal, determined to make a friendly overture there, too. "Nice horse."

She extended her hand. Loco thrust his nose at her. She flinched before realizing that the horse's muzzle was soft and velvety beneath the bristle of whiskers. He didn't chomp at her fingers, but moved supple, leathery lips against her palm.

Denver took her hand and pressed something into it. "Old Loc's looking for a treat. Hold your fingers out straight."

Slices of carrot. The horse gently lipped them up, crunching greedily. He returned to her palm, nostrils fluttering, the nibbling lips smearing her with spittle.

She giggled. "That's ticklish."

Denver clasped her hand for a moment before releasing it. He gave the horse's neck an affectionate slap. "Loc's a good beginner's horse. He'll take care of you just fine."

What about you? she wondered as she rubbed her palm on her jeans. The way he'd touched her had made her ticklish inside, too, even when she reminded herself that she shouldn't take the cowboy seriously.

She stroked Loco's nose. He butted her, scraping her chin with his bony head. Ouch. She pushed him away, her fingers tightening on the rope as the horse threw his head high.

"Steady, boy." Denver lifted a saddle onto Loco's back, then reached beneath the horse to snag the dangling cinch. The motion rippled impressive muscles beneath the clinging tank. In the still heavy heat of the stable, his skin glistened with perspiration.

Alice's mouth felt like cotton. "Are you a real cowboy?"

He straightened. "Worried 'bout how I'll handle your lesson, Allie?" He doffed his hat and raked a hand through his burnished blond hair, studying her.

"I, uh, I've never ridden before."

"No need to fret. Most of our guests are greenhorns. Trail ridin's no challenge at all. You'll do as well as any of 'em once I teach yew the basics."

Oh, boy. She gulped, distracted from the fact that he hadn't answered her question. Maybe she didn't care whether he was genuine.

Denver hung his hat on the saddle horn and finished the tacking up, going off on a rambling, colorful story about riding broncs on the rodeo circuit and winning the silver buckle prominently centered on his tooled leather belt. Alice's eyes dropped to the bulge below it, then darted away. Smirking, he picked up the reins and matter-of-factly took Alice's hand in his, leading both her and the horse outdoors into the glaring midmorning heat.

The riding ring was empty. A couple of horses occupied a nearby corral, dozing in the shade of a stand of cottonwood trees. Denver told her that the rest of them had gone out on the early trail ride.

"Let's get you mounted up." His accent seemed to come and go. He retrieved his hat and set it on his head, tugging the brim low with a devilish, one-sided grin. "I'll turn you into an easy rider in no time."

Alice shuffled in the dirt. Loco seemed enormous to her again, the saddle perched high on his back. She looked uncertainly at the stirrup.

"Y'want a leg up?"

She didn't know why she was hesitating. Riding a horse was nothing to be timid about. Rock climbing or skydiving, yes, but this was a small start. "I want to try it myself."

Denver guided her hands to the saddle, then held the stirrup for her. "Go 'head. Stick a foot in here, take a bounce on the ball of your other foot and up you'll go. Easy as pie."

She was less than elegant, but she managed to haul herself into the saddle. "Yawp," she croaked from atop her perch, hastily sticking her right foot into the stirrup. The ground was a long way down. "What do I do now?"

"Grab the reins. Leave some slack. You don't want to be jabbing Loco's mouth."

The leather reins slithered in her damp hands. The horse's ears flicked back and forth, but he didn't move. "Now what?"

"Y'feelin' okay in the saddle? Got a good grip with your thighs?" Denver's eyes glinted from beneath the hat brim.

Sweat trickled along her hairline. "I think so."

"Then go ahead and squeeze him with your heels."

She prodded the horse. Loco twitched a shoulder and swished his tail, his head hung so low she wondered if he was taking a nap.

Denver chuckled. "Try again."

She dug her heels in. The horse turned his head and rolled an eye at her before lazily picking up his hooves to walk toward the opposite side of the corral. At first, Alice felt a bit queasy at seeing the ground moving beneath her. When she looked up and realized that they were traveling at no more than an amble, she began to relax.

"Follow the rail." Denver stood in the center of the ring with one hip cocked and his thumbs hooked in his pockets. "Get used to his rhythm."

Trying not to apply a double entendre to the words, she concentrated on the creak of the saddle and the bobbing comfort of Loco's head.

They completed one circuit of the ring without disaster. That small achievement seemed significant.

She was doing it. She was riding.

No need to get excited yet. Even the rankest amateur could sit on a horse for a walk.

She wriggled in the saddle, getting more comfortable. Loco felt steady and reliable beneath her, despite his name. She was able to take a look around at the lush green grounds of the resort. Desert stretched way in the distance, sere, brown and strewn with cactus and rock formations. Tomorrow, she'd ride into it, as bold as you please.

When she closed her eyes, she could almost see herself, mounted on Loco, no longer timid or awkward. There was a man riding beside her, sitting tall on a flashy black stallion, silhouetted against the backdrop of the setting sun.

But who was he?

Denver, Alice decided. She inserted his green eyes and easy grin into the picture, but before long the glib cowboy's face transformed into the serious features of Kyle Jarreau.

She shook her head. That wouldn't do.

"Give him a kick with your heels," Denver called. "Get him trottin'."

She settled down to learning to ride. A quick hard squeeze earned Loco's attention. His ears flattened, but he set off at a trot, bouncing Alice up and down in the saddle. She grabbed the saddle horn, not caring that the move branded her as a tenderfoot. She was a tenderfoot.

Loco jogged along the rail. Alice's rein hand jerked in time with the rest of her. She felt as if she was sitting on a jackhammer. "I—I—I'm g-gonna fall!"

Denver only chuckled. "You're too tense. Loosen up. Go with him."

I'm going whether I want to or not, she thought, but she tried to relax her rigid spine while still keeping her legs clamped to the saddle. The trot became easier to handle. More of an eggbeater than a jackhammer.

"Now let go of the horn," Denver instructed.

Let go? Was he crazy? But she eased her grip. Thank God Loco was well trained, continuing to jog in a wide circle regardless of his precarious rider.

"Heels down. Settle yourself low in the saddle."

Alice swallowed. Sweat poured off her. She was developing a stitch in her side from the relentless jostling. But she also felt a flicker of triumph. Horseback riding wasn't so difficult, after all. Maybe she could meet other challenges, too.

"There y'go!" Denver crowed. "Settin' mighty pretty."

She lifted her chin to toss a smile at him. The second her gaze came unglued from Loco, so did her seat.

She fell so fast, she didn't have a chance to save herself. She found herself sitting in the dirt, not sure how she'd got there, except that her tailbone said it hadn't been a gentle trip. Loco had come to a halt in the corner of the riding ring, his reins trailing in the dirt.

Denver knelt beside her. "You okay, Allie?"

"I'm okay." Her jaw ached where her teeth had jarred together. "What happened?"

"Loc put a little giddyup in his stride and you came a-cropper."

"Oh. I fell off?" Apparently her brains had also been jarred. She spit grit out of her mouth. "I fell off while *trotting?* This is so embarrassing."

"Nothin' to be ashamed of." Denver gave her a hand up. "It happens to everyone."

"Even you?"

"Why, sure." He smiled. "More times'n I can count."

Alice wiped her face with the back of a wrist. She

wished again she had a handkerchief. Why did no one carry handkerchiefs anymore? If Denver was truly the total package, he'd have been handy with a bandanna.

"Well," she said, "at least I didn't hurt anything but my pride."

Denver chirruped to Loco. "You game to climb back aboard?"

"Do I have to?"

"It's for the best. Y'can't let fear set in." He caught the reins and led Loco toward her. "Shoot, Allie. I was once thrown hard by a mean ol' bronc name of Twister. Soon's my collarbone healed, I was back on board spurrin' the demon out of that stud. Won me a big old purse in the bargain."

"I could use a new handbag," she said, and Denver laughed, a deep guffaw that sounded more natural than anything that had come out of his mouth till then.

His eyes fixed on hers and she felt an odd familiarity in his steady gaze. "You're somethin' else, sweetheart."

She smiled bashfully and took hold of the stirrup.

"Hold on." He reached behind her and batted at her derriere, releasing a cloud of dust. Heat shot through her when his hand lingered, only for a moment, but long enough to turn her insides molten. "Can't have you ridin' dirty," he said in a low voice. She shivered, despite the fever he'd created. "Not a sweet li'l thang like you."

She bolted onto the horse, mounting with little grace but plenty of speed.

"Eager, ain't cha?" Humor tilted Denver's mouth. He swatted the horse's back end. "Get on, then, Loc. Give our gal a nice smooth ride."

The horse moved off. The cowboy walked in the other direction, talking to himself, though Alice heard every word. "I always did say it's the quiet ones that surprise a man with their enthusiasm, once they get a taste for it."

A TASTE. DENVER'S words had stayed with Alice throughout the day, from her wobbly dismount off Loco after a jittery lope around the ring to her first experiment with a boogie board at the wave pool. She'd lived by the ocean her entire life, but the water in Maine was too cold for swimming or surfing. She'd never gained a toehold in the marina crowd, either, with their fancy sailboats and yachts. Dinghies had been her speed.

I want more than a taste. She dug her spoon into a sweet cloud of meringue. *I want a full-course meal.*

"That looks good." Chloe pulled out a chair and sat opposite Alice. "Hiya. I see you worked up an appetite."

Alice waved her spoon hello. She hadn't felt like getting dressed up, so she'd chosen to dine in the less formal Blue Sage Bistro. "Everything is so good here. I've decided I'm going to work my way through the entire menu, including desserts."

"Why not?" Chloe held up a file folder. "With all the activities I have planned for you, you'll burn off every one of the calories."

"I may resist the mesquite-smoked rattlesnake until the last night, then," Alice admitted.

Chloe laughed. "How did you like the wave pool?"

"It was a challenge. I didn't expect the waves to be so strong. Like a real surf." Alice squirmed, aware of the aches and pains she'd accumulated in just one day. The wave machine had flipped her head over heels several times, until one of the lifeguards had shown her how to coast and paddle on the boogie board. "I'm not very athletic. I got knocked around some."

"But it was fun, wasn't it?" Chloe didn't wait for an answer. "Are you ready for more?"

Alice licked raspberry purée from the corner of her mouth. "Bring it on."

"That's what I like to hear." Chloe consulted the folder. "What do you say to a hike up Camelback Mountain? There's a group leaving tomorrow morning at six."

"That early?"

"You know what they say. Only mad dogs and Englishmen go out in the noonday sun." The sally seemed forced, as if Chloe had used it many times before. She wrinkled her nose. "Okay. The truth is, we have to make adjustments for the summer months. It's our off-season and we're at lower capacity. Most of the guests only want to hang out at the water park." She smiled again. "You're really livening up my day."

Alice took a breath. "All right. I'm game. But I also wouldn't say no if you scheduled me a few siestas."

Chloe dashed off a note. "I'll leave you plenty of downtime. Now, what about cycling? Do you know how to ride a bike?"

"Yes." Alice was relieved that for once she could answer in the affirmative. Bicycles were popular on the island, which was small enough that cars were more of an encumbrance than a convenience. She pedaled the same Schwinn she'd had since she was fourteen, complete with a wicker basket for toting home groceries and buckets of clams.

"Then I'll sign you up for mountain biking. I've gone myself, and it's a super experience, just super. But remember to stick to the marked paths or you might find yourself skidding down a mountainside. The sandstone can be kind of slick."

Alice hadn't counted on biking being an adventure sport. "That sounds fine," she said slowly, "but is there anything I can try that doesn't risk broken bones?"

Chloe considered her lists. "There's trail riding. The horses are very tame. How did your lesson with Denver go?"

"Denver," Alice said. "Wow."

"I know." Chloe giggled like the girlfriend she was rapidly becoming. "Isn't he a hoot?"

"He's a hoot," Alice agreed. "Except I was thinking more about his…um…"

"Good jeans?"

"Yeah." Alice's eyes went to the wide rattan paddles of the fan circulating above the table. The ceiling was painted a cool green-blue. "They were very nice jeans."

"Tight," Chloe said with admiration.

"Is he single?" The question was bold for Alice. She wasn't usually open about being interested in a man.

Chloe's response was emphatic. "One hundred percent."

"A player?"

"Mmm."

"That's what I suspected. I mean, he was flirting. With *me*."

Chloe's brows went up. "Why *not* you?"

"I'm not really the kind of woman men flirt with all that often."

"I don't see why not. You're cute."

Alice did feel as if she'd at least made it onto the "cute" scale, even if she was hovering at the low end. The new clothing she'd bought for the trip was a minor factor. Shedding her Osprey Island persona as everyone's favorite pal and all-around substitute worker was major. She was not nearly as drab and used-up as she'd been feeling the past few years.

Even her mother would have approved. Dorothy Potter had fretted over her youngest daughter's lack of a social life, but she'd wanted Alice close. The small sum she'd set aside in her will as Alice's "mad money" had been a total surprise.

Alice decided to confide. "I did have a drink with Kyle Jarreau last night."

"Kyle Jarreau?" Chloe opened and closed her mouth, emitting only a faint squawk. She leaned over the table. "You're serious? *Kyle Jarreau?*"

"Is that so strange?"

"Hell, yeah. He doesn't…um, well, he just *doesn't.*"

"It was only a friendly gesture." But they'd flirted, or at least Alice had. Unless she'd built their twenty minutes together into a legend in her own mind. "He wanted to welcome me to the resort."

"Ohhh, then, that's different." Chloe still seemed puzzled.

Alice dropped her gaze. "He was nice."

"Mmm. I don't think of him that way, but then, he's my superior. And I'm only a cog in the wheel, far beneath his notice. It's just that I've heard how he's very strict about…"

Alice waited. Chloe's hesitation seemed uncharacteristic.

The young woman blinked. "About everything, I suppose."

Alice was oddly let down. "I sort of had that impression."

"See," Chloe went on, lowering her voice, "it's that Prince Montez has this policy, all spelled out in the employee handbook actually, about how employees are not to 'associate' with the resort guests. Socially, that is. When I came aboard, I was told that engaging in hanky-panky would get me fired. No exceptions. Jarreau's edict. Except for…"

Alice's pulse picked up. Her lips felt strangely tender.

"…workers like Denver, for instance…" Chloe continued with a small grimace, and Alice's expectations sank. They'd been absurd, anyway. Had she really expected Kyle to make an exception for *her?*

"He flirts *very* openly. And no one says a thing. He's practically encouraged, because the female guests like it. Or the servers, for instance, and the pool attendants. They depend on tips, so of course some of them use what they've got to act extrafriendly with guests." Chloe sat back. "But of course no one crosses the line. Not without consequences."

Alice traced a finger along the edge of the waxed pine table. "I see."

"I've said too much."

"No, I'm glad I know. Not that I was taking Denver seriously. He was pretty obvious." Alice flicked her bangs out of her eyes. Kyle was another matter. "But I suppose I *did* like it. I was flattered."

"Sure, why not?" Chloe's smile was a bit strained. "Enjoy the heck out of it. You're on vacation!"

**The cowboy tradition is alive and well in the
American Southwest. Visit the authentic frontier
town, Rawhide, at Wildhorse Pass.**

July 22
Dear Jay,
Well, your big sister made it through her first full
day of vacation relatively intact, except for sweating away about five pounds in the heat and suffer-
ing a bruised ego after a fall—my first attempt at
horseback riding. It's not as easy as it looks to
"cowboy up." Tomorrow they're setting me loose
in the desert for a nature hike. Watch out, cacti and
scorpions!
XOXO,
Alice

CHAPTER FOUR

"INCOMPETENTS." Chef Rodrigo Chavez's florid face was the same pinkish-purple as the sugar flower on the tip of his finger. "I am surrounded by incompetents!"

The resort's catering manager and wedding coordinator exchanged wary looks. Stumbling over each other's words, they tried to salve the chef's legendary temper, which was matched in size only by his towering ego.

A flick of his meaty hand sent the offending sugar flower zinging past the manager's head. It splatted against the kitchen wall. "Puce!" he roared. "I could vomit out a better wedding cake than the tripe you're giving me."

Behind him stood two of his staff, eyes downcast, looking defeated in their aprons and white hats. On the steel surface before them was the product of countless hours of work—the various layers and decorations that would become a wedding cake. Trays of meticulously handmade sugar flowers had been laid out in preparation for the final assembly.

"Puce!" Chavez repeatedly smashed the fragile creations, flattening them to pancakes. "I ask for lavender and these idiots insult me with *puce*."

The chef failed to notice that Kyle, summoned by the catering manager, had arrived through the secondary service entrance.

For once, Kyle had been grateful for the interruption. He'd had trouble concentrating on his work. Two nights in a row now—almost a habit. Dealing with a temperamental chef was a welcome distraction from the idea that he might possibly not be as disciplined as he'd always believed.

"Chef Chavez," he said.

Down went the man's fist. *Bam. Bam. Bam.* Trays rattled as they knocked together. One, filled with arched stems of sugar orchids, tipped over the edge of the counter and crashed to the floor. Everyone but Chavez flinched. The man was as oblivious as a toddler in a tantrum.

Kyle raised his voice. "Chavez."

"Who…" The chef swung around, jowls swaying. Seeing Kyle, he snorted and scooped up one of the iced layers of cakes.

The wedding coordinator covered her eyes.

Kyle had hoped to save the situation; now he saw there was only one way to go. Quick, clean and direct.

"Chef Chavez," he said, "you're fired."

"Fired? Rodrigo Chavez?" the chef sputtered. The cake in his fingers teetered wildly. "I am winner of the Soledad Ecole gold medal two years running. You can't even *think* of firing me."

"Yet, I am." Top-tier chefs were never easy to replace. But they'd had trouble with Chavez before and tonight's scene had made up Kyle's mind. "Leave this kitchen at once."

Chavez's bravado deflated. The cake swayed back and forth. "You're making a mistake."

Kyle shrugged. He fisted his hands so tightly in his pockets, he felt his pulse.

The chef inhaled, getting back some of his bluster.

"Fools!" he barked. "Incompetents!" He whirled, swinging past the corner of the worktable, the cake still held aloft. "I won't put up with it any longer."

Kyle pointed his chin toward the exit. "You know the way out."

The porthole door to the neighboring kitchen swung open, clipping the chef's backside. He lurched, perhaps more violently than the nudge called for. The cake popped off his upraised hand and landed upside down on the floor, despite one of the assistant chef's valiant effort to catch it midair.

"Oh, dear," said Alice Potter in a small voice at the door, a hand clapped over her open mouth. She looked vulnerable and frightened with Chavez looming over her.

"I'm sorry…" she began.

A hotel employee stepped in through the same door, her eyes going from the cake on the floor to the formidable chef to Kyle. "It was my fault, Mr. Jarreau. We were taking a tour of the kitchens and—"

"I cannot work under these conditions." Chavez whipped off his tall chef's hat and stomped out, double chin raised high.

His departure unfroze the rest of the employees. They rushed forward, talking at once about what was salvageable and how they could recover to deliver the wedding cake on time.

Although losing the head pastry chef was a blow, Kyle had complete trust that the staff would come up with a plan.

Alice was his concern. She seemed horrified.

"Don't worry," he said. "It's not your fault."

"But I made your chef quit."

"No, you didn't. I'd already fired him."

"You had?"

"Right before you came in. The man was a tyrant, which is necessary in the position, but too volatile."

Alice blinked. "What? Wait. You *approved* of him being a tyrant?"

"Yes, of course. Tyrants are some of my best employees. But there are limits."

She laughed. "You're an interesting man, Mr. Jarreau."

"Kyle," he said, but she'd already moved past him to help scrape the cake off the floor.

"It was a middle tier," said one of Chavez's underlings in despair. "We'll have to bake a new one, and we won't be able to assemble until it's done." She dumped the pieces in the trash.

"Can't you substitute a cake that's already made?" the catering manager asked. "There must be something on hand." She consulted her clipboard. "Otherwise, there's no chance of finishing on time. It's a morning wedding. The cake has to be delivered by ten-thirty at the very latest."

"Ten-thirty? I don't know, that's going to be close." The curly-haired pastry chef wrung her hands. "It's a custom flavor—champagne chiffon with lime-curd filling. It'll have to be baked from scratch. And then we have all these ruined decorations to redo."

"I can help," Alice blurted into the momentary silence.

The employees looked at her dubiously, Kyle included.

"I'm an experienced cake decorator," she explained. "My best friend has a small bakery back home, and I've worked there off and on for several years."

The catering manager shook her head. "The work we do is a few cuts above your average neighborhood bakery. But thanks, anyway."

Alice looked down at her hands.

Kyle was sorry to see her being summarily rejected, but he couldn't have a guest pitching in. PM wasn't running a charity bake sale.

He drew her away from the employees. "That was nice of you to offer. Unnecessary, but nice."

She lifted her face and he saw that she hadn't been intimidated. She'd been practicing restraint. There was a stubbornness in her eyes. "I could do it, you know. I may not be a highly paid professional, but I'm not an amateur, either."

"I'm sure."

Her eyes narrowed. "Don't patronize me."

The woman who'd arrived with Alice approached Kyle with her hand out. "Mr. Jarreau. Chloe Weston, hospitality."

"Of course," he said, as they shook hands. He recognized her from the previous evening, even though he hadn't placed her by name. The resort employed a staff of two hundred. He met regularly only with the department heads.

"I apologize, sir. I don't usually bring guests into the kitchen, but when Alice expressed a special interest, I thought this once it might be all right."

"No, no. Not your fault," he said, watching Alice, who'd left them to pick up a pastry bag from the worktable. With a few deft motions and turns of the wrist, she produced a puce rose exactly like those remaining on the trays. Rather than call attention to her accomplishment, she set the rose down, found an abandoned rolling pin and lump of lime-green fondant, and began to work again.

Noticing, the catering manager motioned to the assistant chef. They turned to watch as Alice carved pieces out of the flattened fondant. She twisted them into shapes and carefully set them aside. They seemed like nothing special to Kyle, until he compared them to the remaining tray of delicate sprays of lime-green orchids and saw what they would become.

"You know what you're doing," the assistant chef observed.

Alice didn't glance up. "That's what I said."

The chef pointed to the other assistant. "He's Fred and I'm Rivka. Now that Chavez is gone, it appears I'm in charge." She glanced at the other women for confirmation.

"Go right ahead," the catering manager said.

"Be my guest," the wedding coordinator chimed in.

"Hire her," Fred urged. "We could use the help."

"Impossible," Kyle said to remind them of his presence. He was in charge. "Our guests don't work."

"No one asked me to." Alice was matter-of-fact, continuing her activity without interruption. "I volunteered."

"Nonetheless." Even though Kyle knew he sounded pompous, he couldn't stop himself. He never showed his sympathetic side in front of staff, in case they took advantage.

"I can't allow it." He turned a stern eye on his employees. They should know better. "There must be someone you can call in to help. It's only a few sugar flowers."

Alice made a "heh" sound.

"Yes, Mr. Jarreau." Rivka's forehead wrinkled. "Let me think. Julie's on maternity leave and Alex just finished a double shift. They're our top decorators. But I'll manage." Her gaze lingered on Alice's efficient hands. "Somehow."

Kyle walked to the door. "Miss Potter?"

She still hadn't looked up. "Don't interrupt me now."

He hesitated.

He couldn't *force* a guest to obey. But an employee...

With a sharp gesture, he waved over the catering manager. He dropped his voice. "Take care of this."

"Yes, sir."

He walked out, quite dignified, yet still with the uncomfortable feeling that his departure was more like Chef Chavez's than he would have preferred.

In her own quiet way, Alice Potter had managed to undermine him. But damn if he didn't sort of like that about her. She was unassuming but never obsequious. He was a man with her, not a boss.

That was a singular identity he'd set aside for far too long. And maybe *that* was what had kept him up since he'd seen her last.

"THERE WAS THE BRIDE who insisted on bringing in her actual dress as a model," said Rivka, the assistant pastry chef. "We had to pipe icing that matched her lace exactly. And I mean *exactly*. Down to the tiniest thread."

"Ten straight hours of piping." Fred, the other assistant, smoothed fondant over the replacement layer cake. "Your typical cake-decorating siege."

"*Pfft. You* don't pipe. My hands were cramped for days." Rivka glanced up from the lilies she was shading with a minuscule brush and an artist's palette of custom-mixed food coloring. She looked over Alice's work on the sugar roses.

Alice allowed herself a moment to preen. After several of her flowers hadn't passed muster and were unceremoniously scraped into the trash can, she'd learned fast. Rivka was a lot more exacting than Sue. The air-conditioned surroundings of gleaming stainless steel were also a stark contrast to the musty back room of Suzy Q's, where they produced their far more humble cakes on a scarred butcher-block table. The biggest job she'd ever worked on had been a five-tier cake for a society wedding reception held at the Whitecap Inn.

Rivka nodded. "You're doing a good job for an…uh…"

"For an amateur," Alice supplied. "You can say it. I don't mind. Cake decorating is just something I picked up. It's not my career."

"What is, then?"

"I'm a schoolteacher."

After moving in with her mother, Alice had relied on substitute teaching, taking jobs on the mainland whenever she could. But being a teacher was still a strong part of her identity.

She stifled a yawn and squeezed another cluster of rose petals out of the flat-tipped pastry bag. She was accustomed to monotony. But she'd always been careful to hide her boredom from her mother, a sweet soul who'd hated being trouble for others.

Alice yawned again and checked the clock. Almost midnight. So much for her plan to check out the resort's nightlife. They'd been working on the cake for hours, long enough to stop worrying that Kyle Jarreau would return.

She'd insisted on staying.

Because they'd needed her, she told herself, stopping for a moment to stretch her arms. Just like her mother had needed her all those years. Or her brother, Jay, to step in and babysit his kids. And Susan Queeg, the friend who ran the bakery on a shoestring.

Alice was used to being needed. It was easy, even comfortable. Certainly much more comfortable for her than stepping into a nightclub on her own.

"You okay?" Rivka asked.

"Uh-huh." Alice frowned. She'd fallen into old habits at the first opportunity. Here she was, backstage once again. Supporting, not participating.

"What's that like—teaching?" Rivka had finished with the orchids and was now building the cake with Fred's help. They were a Mutt-and-Jeff pair, Rivka short, round and bespectacled, Fred tall and skinny with a goatee and spiked hair, tinged purple. Or puce, as he'd pointed out, holding one of the roses to his chin for comparison.

"Teaching. Hmm." Alice had reached the point of tiredness where her thoughts wandered in all directions. It wasn't difficult to push aside the uneasy sense that she'd taken a wrong turn and was circling around her old life like a hiker lost in the woods. "I haven't taught full-time for a while, but I liked it. I taught elementary school. Fifth grade. The kids were so curious about everything." They'd given her the feeling that her life was an adventure, too.

She sat upright. She hadn't thought through her motives before, but now it seemed obvious that this trip was her attempt to recapture that old feeling of adventure. And the desire remained. She *hadn't* lost her way, only allowed herself to be distracted.

"I couldn't handle that," Rivka said. "Fred's nothing but a big old kid and he gets on my nerves." She placed the top tier, then climbed down from the chair she'd been standing on, stepping back to take a look.

"Crooked," said Fred.

They argued good-naturedly until Rivka caught Alice in another yawn. "You should go. I've kept you too long."

"Thanks, but I'll stay. I want to see this through to the end." She might be an easy touch, but she wasn't a quitter.

"We've only got a few more hours of work, putting everything together. I'll probably get in trouble with the boss as it is, keeping you here this long."

"He'll never know."

"He knows everything," Fred said.

"And he has no compunction about handing out walking papers," Rivka said. She looked leery for a moment. "But I'm safe. We're already shorthanded." She and Fred exchanged a grin. They'd admitted to Alice that they weren't exactly sad to see the back of Chef Chavez.

"Don't count on it," Fred said. "You know the stories."

Alice was all ears. "Stories about Mr. Jarreau?"

Rivka peered at her through the smudged lenses of her wire-rimmed glasses. "Um, maybe we shouldn't—"

Fred was less guarded. "Everybody knows. He's ruthless. He even fired his own—"

"Zip it," Rivka said.

Fred laughed. "You're not the boss of me."

"Ha! I am so the boss of you."

Alice tried to redirect the banter. "I don't want to get you two in trouble, but I'd rather not leave until we're finished." She bit her lip. Why couldn't she be this stubborn about making over her life? After all, she'd come here to be carefree!

Was she fooling herself? Was caregiving her true nature?

Rivka filled a pastry bag with white frosting. "But it's your vacation, Alice. You're supposed to be out dancing."

"I was nervous about going alone." After dinner the night before, she'd gone back to the condo and watched a movie on the flat-screen TV.

Cripes. She might as well have stayed home.

"Fred and I can take you. No vacation is complete until you've seen this guy doing the electric slide in silver disco pants."

Alice stayed to the finish, enjoying the camaraderie even though she did no more than hand Rivka flowers and help transfer the elaborate creation to a cart they rolled to a walk-in refrigerator.

Once they'd cleaned up, Fred volunteered to escort Alice to her condo. By that time they were all dulled by exhaustion. The main restaurant kitchen had shut down hours before.

Rivka gave Alice a big hug. "I'd hire you anytime."

She left through the employees' back entrance while Fred and Alice went out the front, walking through the dark rooms of the restaurant to a hallway and finally into the lobby, which was quiet except for a man at the front desk in bleached shorts, cross-trainers and a raggedy-edged sweatshirt.

Alice's eyes were drawn to him. For one second she thought he was Denver. The crazy notion that the cowboy had been so enraptured by her that he was trying to find out her room number passed through her head. At the same time, she knew that was absurd. She wasn't the enrapturing type. She was the ordinary girl-next-door who never said no to a favor. For all her grand resolutions for this vacation, it was most likely she'd end up marrying a nice guy from home. Maybe a fellow school-teacher. A science or history geek, someone serious and comfortably dull.

Not a cowboy.

Definitely not a corporate executive.

The man at the desk turned and said, "Alice," with alarming intensity.

Fred's Adam's apple bobbed. "Oh, hell."

Alice's toes and fingers went numb, as if her blood had pooled elsewhere. In her hot cheeks, for instance. Her swimming brain. The thought slipped by that she'd been too quick to sell herself short—again.

"Good evening, Mr. Jarreau," she croaked.

He raked a hand through his hair. Gathered himself as his expression became more guarded. "Miss Potter." A beat. "Good *morning*. What are you doing here?" He looked at Fred.

Glared, really.

"Dancing," Alice blurted, even though she rarely lied.

"Dancing," Kyle repeated, clearly skeptical.

"Fred and Rivka invited me to…uh…the nightclub."

"Which one?"

Did that mean there were two of them? Alice had no idea.

"Hoodoo," Fred answered, recovering his wits.

She nodded as if that made sense. From her travel reading, she knew that a hoodoo was a rock pillar, but apparently it was a nightclub, too.

Kyle was not convinced. "Enjoy it?"

"Immensely." Alice was strangely recharged by the confrontation with Kyle. She wanted to show him. Show him what, she didn't know.

"But I'm done in," she said. "I need to get home."

Kyle stepped in, smoothly cutting out Fred. "I'll take her. You must have hours of work to do on that cake." He raised a wicked eyebrow. "Seeing that you chose to go dancing first. With a guest of the hotel, no less. Have you forgotten the hotel's policy against fraternization?"

"They only did it to be nice to me," Alice declared,

realizing she'd gotten the pastry chefs *into* trouble, not *out* of it.

"Won't happen again, sir," Fred said with a caustic tone, adding a "See ya, kid," for Alice while moving at a clip back the way they'd come.

Kyle watched the other man leave. "Funny how you two came from the direction of the kitchens, not the club."

Alice met his eyes. "Yes, funny."

He frowned.

She said no more on the subject and neither did he, other than giving her a hard measuring look as he held open the front door for her. They descended the stone steps and walked past the large fountain, a Moorish star design lined with colorful Mexican tiles. She wanted to stop and dunk her head in the splashing water, but he'd probably disapprove of that, too.

As they left the main hotel behind, the manicured landscaping gave way to a lush garden. A stone path curved into the darkness, where hidden outdoor fixtures threw dramatic fans of light against the spires of cypress and the spreading arms of a grove of olive trees. They entered an oasis of lush acacia and enormous needle-pointed agave and yucca. Low lights dotted the path like fireflies.

Kyle marched along with no appreciation of his surroundings. His face was carved stone.

When the prickly silence became too much, Alice said, "You know I stayed to work on the cake."

"Yes."

"You wouldn't fire them over that…"

Kyle didn't answer. Her throat tightened. Up till now, she hadn't fully believed he was the coldhearted boss of the staff's tales. Chloe calling him a taskmaster had seemed more admiring than actually fearful. As for the chef's dismissal, that had been justified, according to Rivka. But she'd then cut Fred off from revealing the details of some other past firing that had sounded dire.

"I *made* Rivka keep me," Alice said. "They needed the help. You can't blame them for that."

Kyle's stride slowed. "Then who do I blame?" He looked sidelong at her and said, "You?" in a thick rough voice that sent a shiver racing through her.

CHAPTER FIVE

ALICE TOUCHED her tongue to dry lips. "You blame the chef who destroyed their work."

Kyle gave a quick nod. "Of course."

The reasonable capitulation was unexpected. He'd been acting like such a grump.

Maybe his tension wasn't as related to Fred and Rivka as Alice had supposed. She watched him closely as they paused at the edge of the garden where the path rejoined the paved roads that wound around the resort. They were populated during the day with golf carts and scooters bearing the PM logo, but at this time of morning they were empty.

He must have felt her eyes on him, instead of the low stuccoed sprawl of the condominiums. "I had no plans to fire them, even if they had taken you dancing. But I'd like to know why you did it."

"Why I lied? Or why I *disobeyed?*"

His gaze flicked over her. "I didn't say that."

"But clearly you're used to being obeyed."

"By staff. You're a guest."

"Ah. I'm among the privileged."

"Yes."

She sighed. He was so darned correct all the time. It was frustrating.

"Why did you?" he asked again.

"Well, I suppose it was because I wanted to help—" She stopped, swallowing the automatic response.

Why had she so quickly dismissed her resolution to make her vacation an adventure? She'd planned on serving herself a full helping of life. Instead, she'd stuck herself away in the kitchen for the entire evening, doing more of what she did at home. She didn't regret chipping in, not a bit, but the choice was a clear warning of how easily she could fall into old habits.

"I'm a helper," she admitted to Kyle. "I always have been." *But I can change. I* want *to change.*

She just had to figure out how to go about it. Scheduling activities clearly wasn't enough.

"What does that mean?"

"It means my life's been on hold." Which hadn't been entirely because of her mother's illness, Alice realized, although that was the convenient explanation. Easier than accepting that she'd done this to herself because she'd been wounded by her fiancé's rejection. Her mother's situation had simply given her a timely excuse to retreat to the nest.

She stole another look at Kyle. He was as tall and straight and square-shouldered as ever. But somehow more approachable, maybe because of the shorts and old sweatshirt, or the nonaccusatory questions.

Maybe it was the safety of concealing darkness.

"My engagement had been broken," she confessed, "and my mother was seriously ill." Deep breath. "But that's not an excuse. That's life. Everyone deals with these things."

"Some handle it better than others." Kyle inclined his head toward her. "How is your mother?"

She shook her head.

"I'm sorry," he said simply. She felt his light touch on her shoulder, as if a bird had landed there. And then a corresponding solid warmth in the pit of her stomach, like her cat had landed there.

She felt herself smiling. She'd had an aching sense of loss over the death of her mother, but it was good to know she could still feel pleasure, too.

"I'm sure you've had similar challenges to overcome," she ventured, wishing she could lure Kyle into talking about himself.

He shrugged. "Sure."

"Like what?"

"Like employees who undermine my authority with the complicity of the guests."

"Baloney," she said, disappointed. "That's no obstacle for you. I get the feeling you barely have to lift a foot to squash any rumblings from the minions."

"Minions?" His laugh was short but unrestrained. "Am I that over the top?"

She swept out an arm. "Lord of the manor."

He peered more closely at her. "What has my staff been telling you?"

"I picked up a few clues from the upside-down cake and the steamrollered sugar flowers."

"I didn't cause that. I merely solved it."

"No, you finished it. You told the minions to solve it."

"Semantics." One side of his mouth lifted. "I'll concede the point. But, Alice—" again, he touched her shoulder "—*you* are not a minion."

She felt the glow of warmth in her middle again. "Sometimes I forget. Forgive me."

"Nothing to forgive." His hand moved to the small

of her back. They resumed the walk toward the condos. "I was being needlessly hardheaded about letting you help out. Obstinacy is one of my, let's say, personal challenges. I've got a one-track mind."

"A lot of men do." Her insides tugged toward the press of his hand. "But I prefer that to wishy-washy, um, wishy-washiness." Her tongue felt like a fish on dry land. "At least you're direct."

"Unlike I'm guessing, your former fiancé?"

"Yes. No. I mean, he seemed to know his mind very well when he finally got around to admitting that he'd dumped me because I wasn't 'there for him.' Or so he said."

"Not true?"

They'd reached the Spanish portico at the pedestrian entrance to the condo complex. Deep shaded loggias ran along the front of each building. Vines of night-blooming jasmine filled the air with perfume.

"Technically, yes." She was reluctant to talk about Stewart's justifications for his betrayal. "My mother's illness made it necessary for me to be on the island. It was breast cancer. She'd tried to get along on her own, with a lot of help from me and my brother, but the chemotherapy kept her bedridden with nausea. Jay had a family of his own to look after, so it was up to me to move in with Mom. I didn't know I'd be there for the next six years."

Hearing herself, she put off Kyle's reply. "Let's not get into that. I'm on the verge of whining. I don't want to be a whiner." She cocked her head to look up at him. "*You're* not a whiner."

"Maybe I should have done some whining. Not tried to keep everything to myself." Abruptly he cut away from the tantalizing direction of his thoughts. "I suppose I never saw the point of rehashing. Things are what they are."

"Does that mean 'what will be, will be'?" Alice mused.

"Definitely not. We make our own choices."

"That's what I'm doing—taking charge of my own life." She would do better at that tomorrow.

"Good for you."

There was a long silence. Not the kind of silence Alice was comfortable with. Nor the romantic moment she'd fantasized about when she'd dreamed of meeting a dashing stranger on her vacation.

"It's not going that great," she blurted. "So far I've choked down a pound of chlorine, developed several blisters from the nature hike and fallen off a horse."

In a snap, Kyle reverted to his professional distance. "Were you hurt? Were you offered medical attention? We have a doctor on staff. It's no problem to—"

"I'm fine. Still a little sore, but that's all."

"You shouldn't have been working in the kitchen."

"And we're back to square one." She chuckled. "Let it go, Kyle."

Surprisingly, he did. "What happened to 'Mr. Jarreau'?"

"You told me to call you Kyle, and I've decided I prefer it, too."

"Huh. And here I'd been thinking that 'Miss Potter' was rather intriguing."

"Tonight I'm just Alice."

"May I walk Alice to her door?"

"Yes." Anticipation ratcheted up her pulse, but when they reached the Raffertys' condo, Kyle stepped away, instead of coming closer.

"Sleep late," he advised, all professional. "Call room

service for breakfast. Or there's a poolside brunch that serves till one."

"Maybe I'll see you there?" At his silence, she explained, "Seeing as you're up just as late—or early—as I am."

"I'm used to four or five hours' sleep a night." She'd almost convinced herself that there was regret in his voice when he added, "Besides, I rarely mingle with the guests."

And good night to you, Miss Potter.

The Prince Montez Oasis Resort's namesake Oasis Garden is a lush paradise of native flora and fauna all year-round.

July 25
Dear Sue,
Boy, do I ever wish you were here! I have so much to tell you, including that I actually went hot-tubbing at 2:00 a.m. Such decadence. Too bad it was only me and my sore muscles! My condo has a spa in a private courtyard and I couldn't resist after several very long days of activity, including horseback riding (I met a cowboy!), a nature hike and cake decorating (yes, you read that right). More later, I'm heading off to brunch now. Ah, the life of leisure…
Much love to Mike and the kids,
Miss Potter (that's what the staff calls me)

"WHY ARE YOU so grumpy this morning?" Lani asked, coming in with Kyle's coffee. She was dressed in a suit so yellow he wished he had his sunglasses. "I heard about you firing the chef, but a dismissal's never affected you like this before. Even that time with Daisy."

He sipped the coffee. Strong and black, sweetened with a hint of sugar. "I haven't said two words. How do you know I'm grumpy?"

"How long have I been your secretary?" Lani didn't wait for an answer. "Three years and then some, ever since you were promoted from assistant manager." She settled down with her cappuccino. "You think I can't read your body language by now?"

"You read me wrong. I'm just a little tired. I didn't get my usual five hours." *Three* nights in a row.

"Mmm-hmm. I heard all about it. You were prowling the grounds at 2:00 a.m."

Kyle grunted. On any given morning, Lani stopped on her way to the office to chat with the doorman, the front-desk clerk, the housekeeping staff. She called them the PM grapevine. He called them her spies. But since he wasn't above making use of their inside information himself, he could hardly complain when she turned the tool against him.

"I couldn't sleep," he said. "I went for a late workout."

"Then why not sleep in? It wouldn't kill you to come to the office after 7:00 a.m. once in a while."

"I couldn't sleep this morning, either."

Lani's lashes fluttered at him over the rim of her cup. "Insomnia?" she suggested with false innocence.

"Huh."

The secretary grinned. She could even interpret his monosyllablic grunts.

Kyle swiveled around to stare out the windows. After leaving Alice at her door, he'd gone back to the hotel with something other than blood charging in his veins.

Not frustration, exactly, but whatever he'd felt, he hadn't liked it. For one, he wasn't in control. Worse, he'd over-reacted. Alice bailing out the pastry chefs hadn't been that big a deal. He'd come off as pompous and rigid—and she'd tweaked him for it. Rightfully.

So that didn't completely explain his inability to sleep. He'd been out of sorts even before he'd discovered Alice in the lobby with that goofy purple-goateed chef. And while pumping iron at one in the morning wasn't his usual practice, it wasn't unheard of, either. The staff shouldn't have had *that* much to comment on.

Then why was Lani watching him with such a calculating expression? She didn't think he was losing it over one somewhat pesky but otherwise unremarkable woman, did she? A *guest?*

Hell, no. Not him.

Kyle put the coffee aside and pulled over the stack of departmental year-to-date reports. "Are we ready for the nine-o'clock meeting?" He'd called for every manager to attend with their annual reports fully updated. There'd be no surprises when the executives arrived next week. No surprises at all.

Lani clucked her tongue. "You could use a yoga class or two. It'd really loosen you up."

"Not necessary. I can touch my toes."

"I wasn't thinking of that kind of flexible."

Acing the performance review would end his anxiety. He might even feel so relieved that he'd sleep for twelve hours straight.

Kyle pulled at the constricting knot of his tie. Admitting anxiety, even to himself, was not getting him anywhere.

Lani handed him a couple of sheets of stapled paper.

"Today's agenda, hot from the printer." She added a brightly colored card. "And here's your invitation to your mother's birthday party."

That he brushed aside. Open the door an inch and the entire tribe would bust through. He couldn't risk distractions, not now.

Lani made another clucking sound, but he ignored her.

"Thanks. That'll be all for now." He took up the agenda, relishing the crisp paper, the scent of fresh ink, the neat printing and perfectly aligned row of bullet points. The schedule sliced into ten-minute increments.

He had order, action, dedication to one goal. That was plenty.

HUEVOS RANCHEROS sounded exotic, but the dish turned out to be a fancy name for scrambled eggs and fixings plopped on top of a tortilla. Nothing new and different there, until Alice bit unexpectedly into the tomato sauce, which was hot with chile. She cooled her tongue with a gulp of guava juice, then sampled some green stuff that turned out to be guacamole.

The chorizo sausages were somewhat familiar, bringing her back to winter mornings on the island when she was a child. Ocean wind rattling the windowpanes. The house chilly. But the kitchen was always warm, with her mother at the stove making breakfast and Alice at the table with Jay. They were usually teasing each other, squabbling back and forth until the food arrived. Stacks of blueberry pancakes, real maple syrup warmed in a battered saucepan, piles of hot, spicy sausage cakes.

Alice looked out across the golf course. The emerald-green grass was cut here and there with sand traps, which curved into question marks. A border of towering palms with upthrust fronds looked like the frazzled paintbrushes her students had used in the classroom.

Four years after Alice had moved back to the island, so did Jay. He'd given up lobstering after his divorce to become a sort of nouveau hippie vegan potter, claiming his surname was Destiny. His ten-year-old daughter and three-year-old twin boys spent part of their summers on Osprey in happy squalor at Jay's bachelor digs.

As their mother's disease had spread, he'd spelled Alice during the worst periods, giving her some relief from the strain. That had been a help, along with having the children near their grandmother. Alice was the loving aunt, the one who stopped by with new storybooks and took the kids on picnics and babysat whenever Jay needed her. She'd enjoyed it, except for the uncomfortable feeling that she'd settled too easily into spinsterhood.

"Well, well, look what I found. Miss Alice Potter, sitting here all by herself."

"But, oh, you look so pretty in that sun hat," a second woman put in breathlessly.

Mags and Mary Grace from the condos. Alice had crossed their gang's path several times since her arrival but always had a horseback ride or lunch to get to.

The gaudy colors in Mags's kaftan clashed with the orange-red of her boisterous curls. "Darling Alice." Her eyes skimmed the otherwise empty patio table. "How are you enjoying your vacation?"

"Very much. Although I confess I'm a little homesick this morning."

"Buck up, toots," Harriet Humbert said briskly as she joined their group. "We'll take care of that."

Oh, dear. Warily Alice tilted up the brim of the floppy

straw hat she'd bought in one of the resort gift shops. "You're all dressed up."

Mags twirled her long strings of wooden and turquoise beads. "We've a wedding to attend."

"A wedding." Of course—the cake. "How wonderful that you're invited."

Harrie gave a husky laugh. "Who said we're invited?"

Mary Grace raised a finger to her lips. "Harrie. Hush."

Harrie crossed her stringy brown arms over a belted fuschia safari jacket. She wore matching walking shorts with orange Crocs. "We're wedding crashers, not felons."

Mary Grace was turning pink around the edges. She giggled nervously. "The boys refuse to join us."

"But you look like a gal with a sense of adventure." Harrie eyed Alice. "Want to come?"

"I couldn't."

"Heh." Harrie raised her eyebrow skeptically. "Got another lesson?"

"No, but…" Alice was dismayed by her lack of daring. Did she need to take lessons on how to have fun, too?

The thought of the wedding cake put her over the top. She'd love to snap a photo of it on display. Her camera was in her bag.

"All right," she said after one last scan of the remaining guests and the picked-over buffet table. No sign of Kyle. "Why not?"

"Atta girl," Harrie crowed.

The trio led Alice around to an area of the resort she hadn't yet seen, an immense formal garden with covered terraces at several levels and adjacent parking. A spacious gazebo with white lacy fretwork was the focal point. Rows of occupied chairs fanned out on either side of a paved path covered with a long white runner. The floral arrangements that dressed up the area were already wilting in the hot sun.

"We're late," Harrie whispered hoarsely as they slipped into chairs in the last row.

"We always take the bride's side at the indoor ceremonies," Mags confided to Alice. "More of a crowd to blend with. But the outdoor weddings are less formal." She settled herself and gazed at the gazebo, where the bride and groom were exchanging vows, flanked by attendants. "We're lucky it's so cool today."

Eleven in the morning and probably a hundred degrees, even in the shade. That was not cool to Alice.

Several people had turned to examine the late arrivals. One man stared suspiciously. Alice fixed her gaze on the members of the wedding party, copying Mags's innocent expression until the awkward moment had passed. Surreptitiously she wiped away the beads of sweat where her hat met her hairline.

Despite Harrie's occasional caustic aside, spoken out of the corner of her mouth like she was in a spy movie, Alice lost herself in the tradition of the exchange of vows. The beautiful words, the linked hands, the couple speaking from the heart.

"Lovely." Mary Grace sighed as the bride and groom kissed.

"Preggo," said Harrie. And indeed, the bride did appear to be somewhat rotund around the middle. That might explain the hot-as-Hades July wedding.

"Oh, dear," Alice said. "Here they come." She ducked beneath her brim as the guests rose to applaud the perspiring newlyweds parading down the aisle.

"That was a good one," Mags said after the couple

had gone by. She looked at Alice with a honeyed sympathy. "You've never tied the knot?"

"Not yet."

"Three times for me," Harrie put in. "But never as fancy as this. I'm a justice-of-the-peace gal."

"I want a real church wedding," Alice said, surprising herself. She hadn't thought much about weddings since her one and only shot at tying the knot had unraveled.

"Something small, but nice," she added, thinking of a simple ceremony in the rustic white clapboard church on Osprey Island. Handpicked bouquets, friends and family, a cake she'd baked and frosted herself.

Uh-huh. All she needed was a groom.

Harrie winked. "White dress?"

"Or ivory." Alice tried not to sound defensive. She was only thirty-four. No longer the dewy virginal type, but not past the age when a white dress was inappropriate.

"Don't worry," Harrie said. "You've got it going on. You're still a hot young babe."

"But you'd better not wait *too* long." Mags craned her neck, eager to join the milling crowd.

Alice was happy to change the subject. "What do we do next?"

"On to the reception, of course." Harrie rubbed her gnarled hands. "This is the fun part."

"How can we possibly…?" Alice looked at the stirring crowd. Although it was sizable, her companions had a way of standing out.

"Confidence," Mags said. "If we act like we belong, no one questions us."

"Personally, I welcome the curiosity. Gives me a chance to brush up old skills." With a wink, Harrie joined the stream of guests moving toward the terraces, where tables and chairs had been set out beneath oscillating fans. "If anyone asks, I'm the groom's great-aunt Gertrude, just back from an archaeology dig in Egypt." She and Mags marched off.

"Smile and keep moving," Mary Grace advised Alice as she took her arm.

Alice nodded, also planning to avoid all eye contact. "I'm only staying for a few minutes." Long enough to see the cake.

They skipped the receiving line and went directly to where the white-jacketed staff from the resort circulated with tall frosty mimosas and Bellinis. Alice was parched and took one gratefully, if guiltily.

She moved to the edge of the top terrace where an immense fan blasted cool air that lifted the damp hair clinging to her neck. Air-conditioning the outdoors? Now that was luxury.

The bride and groom were out of sight. She felt foolish for hoping to catch sight of them again.

Glass doors opened off the terrace to an indoor reception room busy with activity as final touches were being made to the wedding breakfast. The cake would be in there. Sidling closer, Alice got a glimpse of it, set up on a festooned table at the back of the room.

A commotion distracted her from creeping closer. Somewhere among the guests, Mags was saying in an insulted voice, "I have *never*…"

Alice's stomach dropped toward her knees. Mary Grace scurried out of the crowd, her round face bright pink beneath her silver hair. She pulled on Alice's arm. "We'd better go."

Alice put down her drink. "What's happening?"

The wedding guests parted; Kyle Jarreau appeared.

He escorted Mags and Harrie in a way that might have seemed benign if Alice hadn't noticed the grip he'd locked around their elbows.

"Honestly," Mags was blustering, "this is absurd. Of course we were invited." Harrie only grinned, enjoying the upset.

Alice exchanged a look with Mary Grace. She wished she hadn't hesitated at the woman's first warning.

Kyle stopped at the sight of her. "*Alice.* Not you, too?"

"I, uh, came to see the cake."

"I came for the champagne." Harrie held up a glass. "It's delish."

Kyle's jaw tightened. "Put that down and come along. All of you."

Mary Grace and Alice followed meekly as he marched the other two women out of the wedding reception. Once they were beyond earshot and eyesight, he dropped his hands. "Ladies. Never again, do you understand? This is your final warning."

"Aw, hell," Harrie said, "we didn't harm anybody."

"No? The management has had complaints."

"Complaints? Why would there be complaints?" Mags said loftily. "What nonsense. I make an exemplary wedding guest."

"Only when you're invited." Kyle shooed them along. "Try this again and I'll be forced to employ security to keep you out."

Only Alice seemed cowed. Harrie was practically capering. "Security to keep a few little old ladies out of a wedding party. What a hoot! I never heard of such a thing."

"You're an exceptional case." Kyle's scowl deepened. "Incorrigible woman."

Alice detected a thread of humor in his tone and felt much better.

The three women went off in high spirits, no doubt to gloat to the rest of the Cocktail Shakers about being kicked out of the reception by the head honcho himself. Alice and Kyle strolled more leisurely.

"You've been corrupted," he accused her.

She crossed her arms, holding on to herself. Crashing the wedding had been a small thing, but she felt different inside, as bubbly and light as the finest champagne.

"My corruption might be a good thing," she said, ready to float away.

Was she high after one mimosa?

Kyle let the comment pass. "How did you get roped into their scheme?"

"It was what I said. I only wanted to see the cake." Alice remembered her goopy reaction to the wedding. A blush crept into her face. "I'm sorry. I shouldn't have…I mean, I've never done…never been the type to, you know, flout convention."

"Never mind. You didn't rob a bank." He nodded toward the other women, disappearing around a corner. "I was trying to put a scare into them." He cocked an eyebrow. "I'm not sure it worked. They don't seem to recognize my authority."

"They *are* sort of undaunted."

"You might want to keep your distance."

"What for? I'm already corrupted." Alice laughed. "Never fear, I can handle myself." Which was a disingenuous thing to say when she'd almost panicked at being caught crashing the wedding. She was a boringly law-abiding citizen and probably always would be, but

Kyle didn't have to know that. "I've been in my share of trouble."

"Like what? Illegal photocopying of knitting patterns?"

She inhaled with a gulp. "Ooh." She touched him with her elbow. "Low blow."

Kyle glanced sidelong at her. His smile came easily, creasing the corners of his eyes and making him seem less forbidding. "Sorry. I'm sure you've caused all sorts of mayhem in your time."

"Humph. My time's not over yet."

"I can see that."

He'd stopped and looked at her—in an intriguingly thoughtful way—but she kept walking, putting a skip in her step as she whirled around to face him. She called, "I've got to run! I've got another lesson before the sunset trail ride," while continuing to move backward, without looking, without knowing, for once, exactly where she was headed.

CHAPTER SIX

Sunsets on the Sonoran Desert arrive in spectacular colors. Free shows nightly.

July 26

Hi, Dody and Dylan and Danny!

Greetings from Arizona. Yesterday I went riding in the desert on a horse named Loco. Loco is Spanish for *crazy,* but luckily he's not and we got along fine. At sunset, we stopped to roast hot dogs and marshmallows over a campfire. Then we had a singalong with a cowboy who played the guitar. This afternoon is rock climbing! I'm having a great time, but I miss all of you a lot, and your dad, too.

XOXO,

Aunt Alice

"MAY I HELP YOU, MA'AM? Are you looking for something special?"

Alice faced the salesclerk, a girl too young to look so polished. "Not quite this special."

Everything on the racks seemed to demand a gold or platinum card, but Alice was strictly a standard-issue creditor. "I'm looking for something casual, but slightly dressy, you know? None of the new things I brought with me seem right."

"What's the dress for?"

"Dinner."

The girl's gaze swung to the expensive racks.

"An informal dinner," Alice said firmly. "At least I think so. I know we're not going to any of the hotel restaurants." Denver had been definite about that, probably because they weren't supposed to go out together at all. "There might also be dancing." He'd mentioned music.

"Country music? Line-dancing? That sort of thing?"

"Probably, but I don't know for sure." Alice lifted her shoulders. "You see the problem. I need a nice, versatile outfit." She cast a longing look at the slinky, sexy, expensive garments. Denver was the casual type, but maybe if it'd been *Kyle* who'd asked her out…

"Separates might be the way to go." The clerk's gaze traveled up and down Alice. "Size six?"

"Eight."

"Skirt or pants?"

"Probably a skirt. I'm afraid pants wouldn't look right if he takes me to a nicer place." Except that Denver seemed like a beers-at-the-bar kind of date. What would she do if he showed up in jeans?

Thirty minutes later, after much debate, the clerk had solved Alice's dilemma with a pair of dressy black pants, a matching lightweight cardigan in case the air-conditioning was chilly and a tank top the color of a purple pansy. A delicate beaded design at the neckline added a touch of sparkle.

While folding the garments into tissue, the clerk's eyes lighted on a display of strappy sandals with impossible heels. "What about footwear?"

The amount on the register's digital readout was already frighteningly high. Alice shook her head. "No, thanks. I have sandals." Low-heeled, which was necessary. The group trail ride and then yesterday's beginner rock-climbing outing had given her a new set of sore muscles. Even a long walk around the grounds that morning hadn't completely unkinked her. Perhaps because she'd spent half the walk parked on benches in the shade.

"Jewelry?"

"This is fine." She pulled out her credit card, promising herself that there'd be no other large charges. The traveler's checks she'd brought along would have to suffice, even if that meant she'd have to forgo her journey through the entire dessert menu.

Walking out of the boutique with one of the signature shopping bags bearing the Prince Montez crest made Alice feel as if she truly belonged among the high-class clientele. She swung the bag gaily, too busy goggling at a coterie of new arrivals to watch where she was going.

She bounced off an older woman's solid body. "Sorry!" Alice said, turning so quickly she stumbled. Her shopping bag fell, spilling everything she'd bought across the tiles.

"Let me help," said the woman she'd bumped into.

They knelt and gathered the packages. The woman lingered over the beaded top before refolding the tissue. "Nice threads. Got a date?"

Alice nodded.

"I'm Lani. Kyle Jarreau's secretary."

"Yes, I remember." Alice offered her hand. "Alice Potter."

Lani looked across the lobby at the boutique, one of

several upscale shops in the complex. Her lips pursed. "I shouldn't say this."

The back of Alice's neck tingled.

Lani gave a quick glance over her shoulder. "I love the boutiques here, but their markups are ridiculous. You're better off shopping in Phoenix or Scottsdale."

"I didn't want to take the time. I'm going out—" Alice had followed Lani's last glance "—tonight."

Kyle was there. Suited up and talking in serious tones with a couple who reeked of privilege. A bellman wheeled past a cart loaded with Gucci luggage worth a schoolteacher's annual salary.

For a second, Kyle's eyes skimmed across Alice. His expression and posture didn't change. She might have believed that he hadn't noticed her at all if not for the hot-and-cold shiver along her spine.

"Fast work," said Lani.

Alice tore her attention away from Kyle. "Me?" She blushed. "You've got to be kidding."

"I'm serious. There aren't a lot of single available men around this joint, especially this time of year. Believe me, I've looked."

"I've noticed the lack," Alice said, relieved. "Younger men, that is, like under seventy."

"All too soon that won't be a deterrent for me." Lani touched her silver-streaked black curls. "Too bad the staff is off-limits."

"Yes," Alice said, uncertain if the secretary referred to herself.

"Who's the lucky guy?"

Gulp. Alice didn't have the nerve to tell Lani a lie, even if she'd been able to come up with one. Did she dare tell? Denver hadn't said they needed to keep the date a secret. "Oh, well, it's…Denver." She searched her memory. "I guess he never said his last name. But you must know him. The cowboy who works in the stables?"

"Denver." Lani blinked. "Sure, I know him." She looked at Kyle. "Interesting. I wouldn't have thought he's your type."

"I don't have a type. Denver asked me to go out for dinner and maybe listen to some music, so I said yes." In fact, he'd turned his full charm on her during the trail ride, to the point of a fireside serenade. She'd been flattered and had said yes, even if that meant Denver would be flouting company policy.

She could ask Lani not to tell, but Denver was a big boy. He knew what he was doing.

So did Alice. The taboo lent an air of danger to the date, which played right into her new persona.

"I realize he's a cowboy Casanova," she said, to get that much straight. She wasn't naive. "I'm not expecting anything except a good time."

"Of course. I understand, even if *some* people might not."

Although Lani didn't look at Kyle again, Alice knew he was the someone. But why? Was it the fraternization rule that they were so obviously flouting, or was Lani hinting that Kyle really would be jealous?

Alice preferred the latter.

Laughter built up inside her. At home, she'd never have encouraged two men at once. The only playing with hearts she'd done had been card games with her mother.

Kyle had concluded his conversation. He caught Lani's eye. "You have fun," she said to Alice, giving her a wink. "I'll be discreet."

Discreet? Alice opened her mouth, but all that came

out was "Uh…" There was no way to say that she hoped to make Kyle consider her as more than a guest. On the other hand, she didn't want to get Denver into trouble.

"Must run," Lani said. "The boss probably has a list of special requests from Mr. and Mrs. Fancypants."

Alice fumbled with the string handles of her shopping bag, holding off from looking at Kyle again until he and Lani had reached the elevators. She didn't want to see the professional distance in his eyes. Or worse, disinterest.

But she needn't have worried. He didn't even glance at her.

She turned away with a sigh. There was always Denver, and her new clothes. But somehow the gloss was gone from the evening out. Kyle would disapprove, but only professionally.

KYLE DIDN'T give in until the end of the day. With deliberate intent, he strolled to the outer office and sat himself on the corner of Lani's desk. Nothing odd there. They often wrapped up the day that way, going over tomorrow's agenda. Lani would tell him what she'd planned for her evening and twitter at him about the emptiness of his own.

"So," he said, fiddling with his tie, "did you find that particular brand of sparkling water Mrs. Symon requested?"

"I did. Imported from the Swiss Alps at about a jillion dollars per case. It's being couriered from Phoenix as we speak, gently cradled in a bed of chipped ice."

"Good work."

"I'm afraid the genuine Arctic ice was a no go." Lani smiled serenely and handed Kyle a letter to sign. He used her pen to do it, leaning on one arm, looming ominously above her as she folded the letter and slipped it into an envelope.

"Something wrong?" she asked.

He drew back. "What makes you think that?"

"You didn't even read the letter." She sniffed. "One typo in three years and still you always read every word." She applied a stamp and dropped the letter into the out basket. "But not this time."

"That was a lapse. It won't happen again."

Her eyebrows rose. "I hope not. I might get the idea that you trust me."

"Lani—"

"Stuff it." She poked at his thigh. "What's on your mind, boss?"

"Nothing. Oh, maybe the Symons. You know they're in tight with several members of the board. Including Walmsley, the head of the review committee. Their stay must be perfect. The wife is already bitching because she hates being here in the off-season."

"The staff is fully informed and on the case. The princess won't feel a single pea through her hundred-thousand-thread-count sheets."

He looked around the office. "So."

Lani tapped a shiny nail against her chin. "So?"

"Oh, hell." He stood. "Go ahead, get out of here." He raked his hand through his hair. "Have a good night."

He thrust his fists into his pockets and stood there glowering while Lani made her preparations to depart. He would've sworn she took twice as long as usual.

"I couldn't decide if I should tell you," she said finally, turning back from the door. "But Denver has a date."

Kyle recoiled, as if she'd landed an unexpected uppercut. "Denver? Why are you bringing *him* up?"

"Isn't that what was on your mind?"

"You know it wasn't." Dread leached beneath his skin. "Wait. Why are you telling me that?"

Lani's voice went soft and quiet. "The date's with Alice Potter."

"THAT WAS FUN." Alice slipped her hand out of Denver's and surreptitiously wiped her sweaty palm on the jacket wadded in her lap. She could have blamed the heat, but she knew she was nervous because of the man beside her. He'd been touching her all evening: stroking her hair, tracing a finger along her collarbone, holding her close, holding her hand. Holding her attention because she'd never been out with a man as handsome and glib as Denver.

The attention amused her. Even aroused her. But it was too much for her to handle.

"I don't get out dancing very often," she confessed. They were returning to the resort from Scottsdale.

"You did fine." Denver took his eyes off the road and flashed her a grin. "Once I got a couple of beers in you."

That was true. Worrying about getting caught breaking the rules had made her stiff and uncomfortable until the alcohol had loosened her joints. If she hadn't stopped at two, the touching and squeezing might have been more welcome. Even returned. As it was, the thought of the moment when he'd try to kiss her was melting her into a puddle of uncertainty.

She wanted his kiss, and yet she didn't.

Alice tilted her head back, trying to find a draft. The air-conditioning was on, but it didn't seem to put out more than a tepid stream. Denver might play a cowboy for the guests, but he drove a well-used Ford Fiesta, not a pickup.

"I don't drink a lot, either," she said.

"Damn, girl. What *do* you do?"

"Let's see." Life on the island seemed very distant. "I bicycle and bird-watch. I read a lot and hold game nights and movie nights for friends and family. I garden a bit. I've been collecting shells since I was a kid and sometimes I make artsy-craftsy things with them that I sell at the local gift shop." She squinted an eye at him. "Not very exciting, is it?"

Although Denver withheld comment, she could guess his opinion. He'd been greeted at the bar by a crowd of rowdy revelers. Throughout the evening, tales of his cussin', drinkin' and fightin' had flown fast and thick.

"Got a boyfriend back home?" he asked.

"Two of them. But nothing serious."

His shoved his straw hat to the back of his head, surprised at last. "Two?"

"My nephews. Dylan and Danny."

Denver laughed. He took his hand off the steering wheel and reached for hers again.

She evaded him by tucking her hair behind her ear. "I've been wondering. What happened to your cowboy accent?"

"Whatchew mean, li'l missy?"

"Uh-huh. That's what I thought. Was it all an act, even the rodeo stories?"

"I entered a *ro-day-o* contest once on a dare. Stayed on the bronc for an entire three seconds. Broke my damn collarbone."

"What about the cattle roundups? Where'd you learn the campfire songs?"

"I played guitar in a few honky-tonks in my day, so the songs were no trouble. The rest was acting." He wasn't at all abashed. He tossed her a boastful look. "Damn good, ain't I?"

"I guess." Even though she'd suspected the truth, she couldn't help being disappointed.

"Aw, honey. You're disillusioned."

The way he said *honey* made her feel as if she were spread with it. "I suppose you're not from Texas, either."

"Nevada. We lived in a lousy little mining town up in the mountains."

"Who's we?"

"Mom and Dad. My brother and sister." Denver wiped his face. He sported a five-o'clock shadow that gave him a becoming rough-and-tumble look. She supposed that was also carefully cultivated. "The old man would park us in a run-down shack he'd won from some geezer on a bet, then hit the road, looking for his big break."

"Did he ever find it?"

"We had some good times. Some not so good when Mom had to scramble to feed us." Denver shrugged. "But I don't blame the old man. I leave that to my big brother."

"You sound as though you sympathize with your father. Maybe even admire him."

He gave her that sneaky grin again, sneaky because it slid in under Alice's skin even when she didn't want it to. "I'm a rolling stone myself."

"I'll bet you've been in a few scrapes."

"Some. I've been in lockup. Never got into trouble so bad that I was sent to prison, though."

"Oh." Now she wondered how bad a boy he was. And why he was interested in her. There'd been a lot of women after him tonight. Floozies, her mother would have called them. Big hair, big boobs, big appetites for Denver.

"What's your last name?" she asked.

"I go by Lawless."

She laughed. "Fitting. But what's your real name?"

"Lawless is real enough for now." He recaptured her hand. "Why so many questions, sweetheart?"

"Just trying to get to know you."

He dipped his head, keeping his eyes on the pavement, but his knowing smile sent her senses spinning. "Allie, darlin'. There're much better ways of doin' that."

KYLE KNEW he was as conspicuous as hell, pacing back and forth in the shadowed loggia outside of condo building two. There hadn't been a lot of activity since nightfall, but the few folks who had passed by had stared so hard he thought their eyeballs would fall out. Several blinds had parted and curtains had lifted in neighboring windows. He'd waved.

He checked his watch. Time to give up. Denver might keep her out all night. And he didn't need another night of insomnia.

Still, he stayed. Thinking how he'd never lost sleep or got particularly jealous with other women. Not even Jenna.

How come Alice had him so fired up? He'd told himself he was here to put a stop to Denver's rule-breaking, but that wasn't the entire reason. Alice was like a sliver under his skin. Unnoticeable at first, but slowly working deeper. He'd be rid of her when she went home, but until then...

Finally a car turned in, Denver's battered Ford, rolling past the parking lot to the bricked courtyard that served as a convenient drop-off and pickup area. The engine sputtered and died.

No one got out, but Kyle could see them indistinctly through the dusty windshield. Talking?

Yes, talking. Just talking.

He went still. But it wasn't a stony kind of stillness. No, he was jacked up inside, hyperalert, ready to spring at the first move Denver made.

What for? What business was it of his, just because he couldn't get Alice out of his mind?

Keep it professional, he told himself, knowing full well he'd crossed that particular line the moment he'd staked out Alice's condo.

The passenger door opened and Alice emerged, pushing back her hair. Her arm was slender and her skin ghostly pale in the moonlight, exposed by the tiny top she wore. Barely wore, held up only by narrow strings, with a sparkle where it scooped low across her breasts.

Now was the time for Kyle to speak. Let them know he was there. But he couldn't. His mouth was dry, his tongue thick.

Her shoes clacked across the courtyard. The iron gate of the portico creaked open. Denver slunk through it right behind her, reaching out to catch her by the waist and nuzzle her neck.

She let out a laugh and darted away, arriving beneath the loggia faster than Kyle had expected. He was caught out in plain sight.

Her eyes went round. "Kyle!"

He stepped forward. "Good evening, Miss Potter."

"What the…" Denver planted his green cowboy boots and stared, his arms crossed in a belligerent posture Kyle recognized. "What're you doing here?"

"Shouldn't I be asking you that?"

Denver sneered. "Like hell you should."

Alice's head was on a swivel. "What…?"

Denver jabbed an accusing finger. "His goal in life is to keep me from havin' a good time."

Kyle was fighting the adrenaline charging through him. He didn't dare move a muscle. "It's good to have goals," he managed to say through gritted teeth.

"This is my fault," Alice said. "*I* asked *him*. He was doing me a favor. Just as part of his job…" Her voice trailed off.

Kyle's eyes went to her. Did she really care enough about Denver to lie to protect his job? Or would she have done the same for any of the employees, just as she'd defended the pastry chefs?

He shook his head. "You don't have to cover for him."

"I'm not. I'm—" She cut herself off. "Please, Kyle. Don't fire him."

Denver scoffed. "He's not gonna fire me. He hasn't got the balls."

Alice gasped.

Kyle's muscles bunched. "It's within my rights."

"Rights?" Denver laughed. "Yeah, you did it to Daisy, right? Single mother and all." He turned to Alice. "This guy's a cold son of a bitch, I tell ya. Blood's not gonna stop him from doin' that fancy-ass job of his."

Suddenly Kyle found himself an inch away from Denver's face. "Shut your mouth." He was hoarse.

Denver flicked off his hat, his eyes blue flames. "Fire me."

Kyle had raised a hand, ready to defend himself. He clenched it, instead, swallowing hard.

"Do it." Denver breathed heavily, smelling of beer. "Make up your mind, *Mr.* Jarreau. Hit me or fire me. I don't care. Just do it."

Kyle glared. Visceral instincts clawed at his control,

demanding action. But he was too aware of Alice in his peripheral vision, watching them, her face white and her arms clutched across her chest.

He dropped his hand. "Get out of here."

Denver drew back. He swooped up his hat, set it low on his head, hooked his thumbs in his belt loops. "Yeah, that's what I thought."

Kyle's blood drummed in his ears. His mind whirled, taking him back to arguments at home when he'd been a kid. If he stayed very still, if he made no sound, if he counted to a hundred million, the fighting would be over. He could do his homework in peace and quiet.

Denver shot a two-finger salute at Alice before swaggering toward his car. "See ya, honey."

Kyle's head cleared. *No.* He wasn't done.

He caught up, grabbing Denver's shoulder on the other side of the gate. "You will *not* take her out again. Try it, and I *will* fire you."

Denver wrenched away. He kicked the gate closed between them. "I never wanted this damn playacting job in the first place."

"No, you wanted a handout," Kyle said, talking so low his throat ached. Maybe he should have taken the easy way out and given Denver the cash. He'd been a burr under Kyle's saddle since the day he'd strolled across the Oasis lobby as if he owned the place.

"Cheap bastard." The insult was not new. Denver got into the car, cocking his chin at Kyle. "What're you saving it for, anyway?"

Kyle stepped through the gate. "You'd rather be poor? Scraping by from one job to another?" He went up to the car, needing to see Denver's face, to know if there was anything left between them. "Sound familiar?"

Denver didn't answer, except to turn on the ignition. He revved the engine several times, probably scaring residents out of their beds.

Kyle thumped the window. "Get out of here."

Denver was laughing as the car roared away.

Kyle took a deep breath and turned back to the condo complex.

Alice. She hadn't moved.

He walked up to her, his hands hanging limply at his sides. The confrontation had sucked every shred of emotion out of him.

She stood in front of her door, fingers around the purse and jacket she held against her abdomen. "I don't understand," she whispered. "What was that about?"

He regretted the entire event. "I don't want my staff dating the guests."

"All right, but there's more to it than that."

"Never mind." He turned to go.

"Oh, no, you don't!" Her vehemence stopped him. "That was quite a scene. You owe me an explanation."

He rubbed his temples. "It's a long sad story."

"Give me the short version."

He exhaled, then swung around to face her. The concern on her face reached into him, but he shut her out the same way he'd avoided emotional complications since the day, at twelve years old, he'd given up on his family.

"Denver's my brother."

CHAPTER SEVEN

"YOUR BROTHER," Alice said. "Denver is your brother. I don't believe it. You're nothing alike." But hadn't she noticed a resemblance, just a hint of one? Now that she knew, she could see it more clearly.

At that moment, though, Kyle looked nothing like the cocky cowboy. He was a man defeated. She'd never imagined Kyle this way. He'd seemed practically invincible.

"It's the truth," he muttered. He straightened to stare off across the courtyard. His shoulders moved uneasily, as if he had to work the tension out of his body. "He's my brother."

"Yes." As if he needed *her* agreement. She paused. "What was all that about—the fight?"

"Family history. You know how it is."

She remembered what Denver had said in the car on the way home. The absent father, growing up poor. She had a hard time connecting that sort of past to Kyle and his current success.

Unless that was the reason for it.

"I gave him the job here." Kyle's tone was remote. He could have been talking to anyone. Or no one. "I thought, if for once he had stability…" He shrugged. "I thought I was helping. But he only resents me for it."

Alice looked away. She shook the wrinkles out of her jacket and draped it over her arm. Kyle's turmoil was a private thing. "I'm sure he appreciates the job. A lot of people have trouble expressing gratitude."

Kyle snorted. "No. He resents me for making something of myself."

"Maybe he feels…" She reached out, then stopped when Kyle moved away.

There was a long silence. He exhaled and crossed his hands at the back of his head. He clenched his fingers in his hair before dropping them as if they were too heavy to hold up.

"I'm only a bystander," Alice said softly, "but it makes sense that he's jealous."

Her thoughts turned unexpectedly toward her own life. There'd been times when she'd felt green over Sue's good fortune—having it all with the husband, the kids, the cake shop. Or Jay, who'd remained happy-go-lucky even after his divorce.

Fortunately, Sue was a good friend. And Jay had sympathized with Alice's occasional frustration at being stuck on Osprey Island. Her resentment hadn't festered.

It seemed that the Jarreau brothers weren't as lucky.

"Jealous of what?" Kyle said.

"Your…" She couldn't say it was his lifestyle, when she didn't really know how he lived except that he seemed to have all the trappings of wealth. "Your success."

"Denver's never wanted that, not if he had to work for it. He's more like our father."

"A gambler."

Kyle swung around. "How did you know?" His tone was almost accusatory.

"Well, I…it was something Denver said."

"The man claimed to have won and lost millions," Kyle said bitterly. "Wild exaggerations, but for sure he could never seem to hold on to a dime."

Alice realized that he'd taken her comment literally. She'd been envisioning Denver and his father as devil-may-care vagabonds, risk takers, gambling with their futures rather than cold hard cash.

"I'm sorry," she said.

"For what?"

"That you had it so hard growing up. Denver told me some of it. And I understand. My dad passed away when we were teenagers, without much insurance, so we had some lean years on the island before…"

She trailed off. Kyle was looking at her narrowly. She crossed her arms.

"You and Denver got close, huh?" His voice was low. "You enjoyed your little date?"

Needles pricked at her skin. Was he baiting her? Was he *jealous*—the way she'd foolishly wanted him? She didn't care for the reality of that.

"Denver knows how to have a good time," she said carefully, keeping herself occupied rooting in her purse for the door key. Kyle might have a legitimate reason to come down on his brother, but he had no rights over *her.* "We danced. He held my hand."

Kyle cleared his throat. "Did he kiss you?"

"That would be telling." She was emotionally confused, all mixed up about what she wanted. Who she wanted.

Denver was easy, in so many ways. Kyle was complicated.

She refused to play one brother against the other, especially when they were already at odds. Yet it was difficult to know how to respond when she wasn't even sure what she felt.

Kyle had come here, waited outside the condo for who knew how long. He'd intended to ruin her date with another man, but had hidden behind "professional" reasons when he might—just possibly might—have other-than-professional feelings for her.

It was too much.

But hadn't she wanted too much, after years of too little?

Kyle was suddenly only inches away. The heat of his body confused her even more. "Don't kiss him."

She faded back, found the solid door behind her. "What does it matter to you?"

Don't say it's your job. Don't say it's only business.

His eyes were dark and unreadable. The pause while he formed his answer was excruciating.

"I'd rather—" He cleared his throat again. "I'd rather you were kissing me."

Stunning. She was hollow; her insides had dropped away like a stone falling off a cliff. Only one thought stayed in her head: beware of what you wish for.

Her lips seemed to be stuck together. They made a small sound when they parted. "Kiss *you?*"

"Yes."

He touched his forehead to hers, repeated the incredible words with his voice so husky it sent shivers across her skin. "Kiss me."

"That's…that's n-not…"

His hands closed around her upper arms. He held her as if he never intended to let go.

She shut her eyes. Her knees were giving out. "You can't do this. You can't kiss me."

"I can."

"No." With a supreme effort, she battled back the headiness of being admired, sought, *wanted.* "It's company policy, isn't it? What's wrong for Denver is wrong for you, too."

She spun and jammed the key into the lock, then slammed the door behind her without looking back— because she wasn't at all certain she shouldn't have kissed him exactly as he'd wanted.

And damn the consequences.

"HOLD UP," Kyle called, breaking into a sprint. The heat was oppressive even at eight in the morning, but a guy with a gold chain around his neck and a serious addiction to men's hair dye was heading over to take the wheel of Alice's two-passenger ATV.

He put his hand on the vehicle. "Sorry, bud. I'm taking this one."

Alice gaped at him, holding one of the soft-sided coolers the guide had passed out to the small crew gathered for the desert trek.

Kyle nodded at her. "I know the lady."

She stowed the cooler and other gear in the back compartment, keeping her hands busy while she glanced at him. "Shouldn't you be working?"

He snapped the tie-downs into place. "This *is* work. I'm evaluating our selection of off-season activities. Doing quality control. Researching ways to encourage greater participation. Whatever you want to call it."

"Uh-huh." She lowered her sunglasses. Her small smile was touched with a hint of wicked intent. "Why don't I drive?"

"But—"

She tut-tutted. "None of that, Mr. Jarreau. Your guests must come first." Coolly, she slipped under his arm and clambered into the off-road vehicle, a red Polaris RZR. "I'm driving."

"As you wish, ma'am." Teeth clenched, he walked around to the opposite side. The other Razors were now ready to go. The guide made sure the seat belts and safety nets that prevented passengers from catapulting out of the open vehicles were fastened. Engines were gunned.

Alice's expression had grown slightly grim. "Ready?"

The guide dashed over. "Mr. Jarreau! I didn't realize—"

Kyle took hold of one of the bars of the roll cage and vaulted into the ATV. "Surprise inspection."

The guide's face was red. "You could ride with me and I'll—"

"No, no." Kyle waved him off. "This is fine. Treat me as any other guest."

"Yes, sir. First class all the way." The guide called for the group's attention, fumbling with a map as he reeled off the same instructions he'd given in the safety class.

Kyle watched Alice tap her foot impatiently. She wore flat-soled sandals and a pair of jean shorts. The sleeves of a white cotton blouse were rolled above her elbows, with a red bandanna looped loosely at the open neck. Her legs and arms had become lightly tanned. As had the expanse of midriff exposed by the knotted tails of her shirt. He wondered if she wore a bikini poolside.

He rubbed his palms. "I hope you don't mind me hijacking your ride."

"It'd help if you admitted your real intentions," she

replied. "I know you're all business—*supposed* to be—but your excuse was flimsy."

Sunshine bounced off the spotted windshield. He put on his sunglasses, making a mental note to have the Razors washed more thoroughly after every outing.

What *were* his intentions?

He hadn't liked it, not one bit, but by morning he'd had to admit that he was fortunate Alice had saved him from making a big mistake. He'd also admitted to himself that the confrontation with his brother had been born out of jealousy—on both sides. He and Denver had never had a direct rivalry over women, but seeing his brother pulling his "ladies' man act" on Alice had fired up Kyle's desire to protect her. Perhaps to claim her. Once unleashed, the primal urge hadn't been easy to subdue, even after she'd shut the door in his face.

Might explain the impulse to join the desert ATV tour. No surprise, Lani had just happened to know Alice's plans for the day, via her grapevine.

Alice had tilted her head at him. At the corner of her sunglasses, he saw the flicker of her lashes.

"No ulterior motives," he professed. "I'm just along for the ride."

"I find that hard to believe." She snapped the seat belt, turned the key and put the Razor in gear. Every move was neat and economical, accompanied by the bob of her short ponytail. "But if you insist…"

He looked at her. She looked straight ahead through the windshield, smiling faintly while the guide droned on.

Kyle cleared his throat. "Uh, do you know what you're doing?"

She thrust out her chin. "You bet."

He just had time to grab a brace before she jammed

her foot down on the gas and they took off in a shower of dirt and pebbles, rocketing past the rest of the group.

Alice let out a whoop. "Enjoy the ride, *Mr.* Jarreau!"

"WHOA," KYLE SAID as Alice aimed the Razor at a slanted wall of rock. The tough little vehicle climbed without protest and within minutes they'd crested. A glorious panorama of desert opened up before them. She turned the wheel sharply, pulling to a jarring stop well back from the edge of the canyon.

They both inhaled at the expansive sight of the butte dropping away in sheer stone cliffs. A red-tailed hawk soared across the sky, the only movement in the vast stillness.

"We have to go back for my stomach." Kyle removed his sunglasses and wiped his hand across his forehead, smearing the dust and sweat into a brown streak. "It fell out at the bottom of the hill."

"Ha." She climbed out of the vehicle and walked toward the edge. Red sandstone sheered off into a deep, graveled arroyo swagged with bushes she recognized as creosote, cholla and Mormon tea, thanks to her field guide.

He followed. "Where did you learn to drive like that?"

"My brother. He uses an ATV on the island." She glanced fondly at the Razor, its flashy red panels now dulled by dust. "Nothing so spiffy, though." She gestured at the rolling landscape rimmed with craggy peaks. The sky was a bright blue with dark-bottomed thunderclouds high to the west. "And we don't have this."

Kyle shaded his eyes with his hand, scanning the horizon. "Yeah, it's impressive. But you must have quite a view on Osprey Island." Lines fanned out from his squinting eyes. "I mapped it online," he confided.

"You did?" She touched the back of her hand to her cheek. The skin was hot, tender, even with all the sunblock she'd applied. "Why?"

"I like to know things."

She laughed. "'I like to know things'? You sound like one of my fifth graders."

He pushed his hands into the pockets of his shorts, chuckling. "So you're a teacher."

"I used to be. I'm going back to it this fall, I hope. I'm waiting to hear about a couple of jobs I interviewed for, but I don't know. There weren't many openings and the competition was tough." Going up against the peppy young teachers fresh off their degrees, she'd felt like a piece of stale bread forgotten in the cupboard.

"You'll stay in Maine?"

"Maybe. I'm considering Vermont or upstate New York, too." His question made her wonder why she hadn't been more venturesome. This was her chance, finally, to go wherever the whim took her. "I guess I was thinking I should stick close to my family. But…" She gazed across the amazing vista of the desert, energized by its unfamiliarity. "It wouldn't hurt to widen my horizons. I'm learning how invigorating change can be."

"Up to a point. I've moved around a lot with Prince Montez, working my way up the corporate ladder, and after a while, well, you start to long for permanence."

"Really? You seem like the ambitious young executive, dedicated to the job 24/7. Always on call. Ever the professional."

"Right. That's me." His mouth quirked.

"Where's your family? I mean—" she raised her eyebrows "—the *rest* of them."

"Still in Nevada. My sister lives with our mother just

over the border, in a small town called Elk River. We're not close."

"And your father?"

"Haven't heard from him in years." Kyle moved away, his mouth turned down at the corners. "We really should go back. The others will wonder what happened to us."

"There's no rush. The guide said we could go where we wanted, as long as we stayed on the trails and didn't wander too far away." They'd left the group behind at least a mile back, in an area of low rolling dunes where the driving was great fun, extremely dusty, but not very challenging.

"Except you *didn't* stay on the trail. And we're not even within sight of the group."

She tossed her head. "So what? There's a map in the Razor. I know exactly where we are." She grinned. "I bet you always colored within the lines, didn't you?"

"And measured my margins with a ruler."

"I know what that's like." She remembered his happy shout when the Razor got some air, shooting over the dunes. And how he'd egged her on when they'd led the group on a wild ride along a straightaway. "Thanks for lightening up with me."

"It was a helluva ride."

"We're not done yet. Come on." She reached to tug on his arm, but somehow ended up with his hand, instead. "I think I saw some saguaro cacti back in the other direction. If you take my picture with one, I can cross another item off my list."

Kyle checked his watch. "We'll have to hurry. I don't like the look of those clouds. We might be in for a monsoon. The wind and sand can be wicked out here if you're outdoors without shelter."

Alice ignored him. She was thinking how she'd like to rip his watch off and toss it into the canyon. A flash flood might wash it away forever.

"I'm not worried," she said. There'd been several short hard rainstorms since her arrival.

"You should be. The desert is a dangerous place for the—"

"I know, I know! There are rattlesnakes and scorpions." She laughed. "Rock slides and flash floods. Drama and danger at every turn." She even skipped a little as they approached the ATV.

He squeezed her hand before releasing it. "You almost sound like you're inviting disaster to make your vacation more memorable."

"Well...not really. I don't want to be hurt." Out of nowhere, the truth of the innocent comment socked her in the solar plexus. The more she knew Kyle, the more she liked him both as an attractive man and a friend, which meant that her emotions were becoming involved. If that happened, she would be hurt when her vacation was over, she just knew it.

She skidded on the pebbles. He caught her arm. "You okay?"

She sucked in a gulp of the hot air and nodded. "Sure." On the island, she breathed cool moisture, sea brine, the spicy aroma of the pines. She kept her feet on the ground. Her balance never wobbled.

"I'm driving," Kyle said.

She agreed. *Get a grip. You're reading too much into a whole lot of nothing.*

He helped her into the passenger seat. She liked his courtly manners, the care he took with her. The evening with Denver had been fun, too, but in a different way.

On the drive home, he'd sung along with the radio and howled with the coyotes. Mostly as a result of all the beer and whiskey chasers, but the exuberance had been infectious.

She gripped the T-bar under the dash, expecting a hairy ride down the steep hillside. But Kyle only picked up speed when they were on flat ground again.

He glanced at the approaching thunderheads. "Look at that. I told you. There's going to be a storm any minute now."

Earlier, they'd put up the roof of the vehicle to protect them from the sun. But it wasn't enough against rain, especially with the open sides. "A little rain won't hurt us," she said confidently.

A gust of wind rattled the roof covering. "It's not the rain that'll get you, it's the wind and the sand." Kyle swerved off the course she'd set to reconnect with the trail.

"Where are you going?" Less confidence.

"See the cliff face? We'll have better shelter there. We can wait out the storm."

The sand had risen up around them, whipped by the wind. She coughed, choking on the grit. "Pull your bandanna over your face," he instructed. "Your sunglasses will help protect your eyes. Do you have a jacket?"

She spoke through the cloth. "A windbreaker in the back."

"Hold on." He sped toward the rocks, dodging the hoodoo rock formations and bucketing in and out of gullies. She ducked down behind the windshield as they were pelted by the stinging sand. A dust devil spun across a span of open ground, spitting fine gravel. She watched in amazement.

The Razor climbed a steep hill to reach the canyon

wall, well out of the path of flash floods. Kyle parked beneath a thick overhang of rock, then reached into the rear compartment to haul up the cooler and her tote. In short order, he had her wrapped in the windbreaker, the hood pulled taut around her face.

Raindrops began to pelt the vehicle. They were tiny and sharp, but preferable to the sand. She pulled down the bandanna. "What about you?"

He'd turned in the seat to keep his back to the rain. "I'm fine."

"Take this." She yanked a sweatshirt out of her bag, thankful she'd gone through the desert survival guide she'd found in the Raffertys' condo and packed accordingly, no matter how silly it seemed to lug along so much extra clothing. "And this." A baseball cap.

"Thanks."

The rain continued to pound the earth in nearly vertical sheets. They were soon soaked through, despite their attempts to huddle together. She drew her knees up to her chest and wrapped her arms around them.

Kyle's body was warm, his encircling arms a comfort. And then after ten minutes, the rain began to abate. He put his mouth near her ear. "How are you enjoying your vacation, Miss Potter?"

She lifted her head, bumping first his nose, then the hat brim. Despite the chill and the damp, their circle had become almost steamy. "The extremes are really quite extreme," she said primly.

He chuckled. "You should come back in the spring for wildflower season. We'd treat you more gently then." The rain had stopped as quickly as it started, but he didn't loosen the embrace.

"Next time," she whispered, wishing she knew whether there'd be a next time. There could if she made it happen.

"What do you have planned for the rest of your stay?"

"Some people at the condo have invited me out for a day of boating and barbecue. Then there's a dawn hike up Camelback and mountain biking. Chloe says I should go skydiving. I say she's nuts."

"Hmm. Don't forget—the spa is running specials. No exertion required."

"You still think I'm the spa type?"

With one finger, he scraped a strand of wet hair off her cheek. His breathing rasped in and out. "Not so much at the moment."

Her heartbeat drummed. "I'm sure I'm a mess," she whispered, tingling at his touch. She waited a couple of seconds that seemed like minutes. "You can let go now."

"Not yet. We have unfinished business."

She went still, except for the pulse that thrummed through her body.

He prodded her chin until she raised it. "You owe me a kiss."

"I don't *owe* you."

"No, you're right there, but will you give me one, anyway?"

She wanted to. Achingly. "What about company policy? What about Denver?"

"I won't tell if you don't."

"A secret." Forbidden. Clandestine. Illicit. She turned the concept over in her mind. Not the stuff of her romantic daydreams, exactly, but there was a certain appeal. A vacation-fling appeal.

She'd expected *that* kind of move out of Denver.

"Just a kiss," Kyle said. He stopped stroking her cheek.

She was losing him, thanks to her hesitancy.

Alice turned and seized his face between her hands. She laid a bold juicy kiss on him. Their lips smacked loudly. Not the stuff of her romantic daydreams, either, but it'd do.

He smiled, and she was dazzled to discover that she felt the smile through her palms. It traveled up her arms, spread a sweet balm across her nervousness.

"I'm not a number to be crossed off your list," he said.

She blinked.

"And I'm not a challenge to overcome."

"Of course not. I just thought…"

"You'd take the matter into your own hands?" He was still smiling, telling her that even her awkwardness and uncertainty were all right.

She started to take away her hands, but he said, "No, don't move." He caressed her face. His gaze wandered across it before landing, significantly, on her lips.

She licked them. She and Kyle were intertwined. Cocooned in heat and humid desire. He was, after all, the stuff of her romantic dreams.

Light filled her when he placed his lips over hers. Like the sun beaming out from behind a thundercloud. There was a grittiness to the kiss, seeing as they were both covered in a fine layer of sand, but everything else about it was as sweet and soft and smooth as a summer breeze.

Kyle was, without a doubt, a great kisser. The end of their kiss, the end of the vacation, even the end of her loneliness, were the furthest things from her mind. For now, the moment was enough.

At least they rested their cheeks together. Rain dripped from the stone wall. A lizard skittered along the wet pebbles of the wash.

"We should probably start back," Kyle said after a while. "They might be looking for us."

Reluctantly, they broke apart. She found the cooler, shoved into leg well of the ATV, and offered him a bottle of water. They drank, then used her bandanna to wash the sand off their faces and necks. She broke out the packets of trail mix, peeled and sectioned an orange. It was absolutely the sweetest and juiciest orange she'd ever tasted.

They chatted about nothing special. Afterward, she couldn't remember what they'd said, except for being certain that not one word was about hotel policy or Denver.

Jeeps, ATVs and dirt bikes are favorite desert transports for the adventurous set. With its hundreds of miles of trails, the terrain of the Sonora is open for exploration.

July 28
Dear Jay,
It's me again, Miss Adventure. Hee! Did you or Dody read the twins my last card? Since then, I've upgraded from four-legged transportation to four-wheeled. When I get back, I'll tell you all about the tricked-out Razor I drove up a mountainside. And the amazing people I've met.
Wish you were here!
Al

CHAPTER EIGHT

SINCE THEIR DESERT kiss, Kyle had stayed away from Alice for fifty-seven hours and thirty-two minutes. He wasn't counting the seconds. Despite Lani's prodding, he hadn't talked about her, either. When his secretary had gleefully reported that he'd been seen at the condos, he'd played that off as a "meeting" with Denver. Just as his off-road outing had been quality control. If Lani knew that he and Alice had disappeared for an hour on their own in an ATV, she, for once, hadn't had the cheek to question him.

He wasn't as lucky with Gavin.

"Smooth move." Gavin looked down at Kyle on the weight bench and laughed. "Real smooth. The old let-me-save-you-from-the-storm ploy. Let-me-shelter-you-in-my-arms-of-steel. Yep. Works every time."

Kyle's arms seemed made of linguini now. He clenched his jaw and pumped out three more reps before allowing Gavin to take the barbell and replace it on the stand.

He needed to play this off, too, but somehow he couldn't do it. The fifty-seven hours and thirty-two minutes had weakened his resolve.

He blotted his face with a towel and heard himself saying, "That's not the way it was."

"That's the way it always is."

"Alice is different."

They switched places. "I'll give you that point," Gavin said, straining against the weights as Kyle spotted. "From what I hear, she's Jenna's complete opposite. Not that there's any significance to that."

Jenna Malloy was five-eleven, blond, slim, every inch the high-fashion model she aspired to become even though this was Phoenix and she was mainly booked for catalog and local advertising work. Kyle had dated her casually for three months last spring.

"Jenna who?" he said.

Gavin grunted. "You know, that high-maintenance chick who was supposed to be your perfect relationship."

At the time Kyle's idea of perfection had been a beautiful and sophisticated woman who was as detached from real involvement as he was. He wasn't sure when that had changed, but it must have, because Alice was no Jenna.

Gavin finished his reps. Kyle unclamped the weights, considered dropping them on his friend's head.

"What are you harping at me for?" Kyle placed the forty-pound weights in a neat row, then the twenties. "You've been singing the praises of making a commitment ever since you got down on one knee to Melina."

Gavin sat up. "Yeah, well, we're coming up on our seven-week anniversary, and you've had no action of significance in longer than that. I'm getting bored."

"What are you saying? The honeymoon's over already?"

"Not over. We're just kind of settling in, you know? Mel's stopped thinking my whiskers in the bathroom sink are cute."

Kyle cuffed Gavin's shoulder. "Came to her senses, huh?"

"It had to happen." Gavin sighed forlornly. "No more

elaborate home-cooked meals, either. Goodbye souvlaki and that custard-pie thing with phyllo. I gained five pounds and she gained three. We're eating healthy from now on."

"Damn, man. That sounds hellish. I really feel for you."

"Yeah, yeah, yeah."

They walked to the utilitarian staff-only locker room, which was unoccupied and silent as a tomb except for a drip in one of the shower stalls. Kyle worked the padlock on his locker. "They say the first year of marriage is the hardest."

"Thanks, Dr. Phil." Gavin had brought a basketball in with him and proceeded to bounce it on the tile floor. The sound ricocheted around the room. "How about a few games of horse before we go?"

Kyle looked at his watch. "Where's Melina?"

"Out with the girls. She's 'reclaiming her independence,' whatever that means."

"That means you should be waiting for her at home. With a big bunch of flowers and the bed turned down."

Gavin's brow furrowed.

"She'll be tipsy," Kyle explained.

"Hey, that's right." Gavin brightened. "The honeymoon's back on, baby."

Kyle yanked off his T-shirt, then took out a towel. He glanced at his watch again. Fifty-seven hours, fifty-five minutes. That ought to be long enough to prove he wasn't smitten like a schoolboy, despite his recent ill-advised actions. He'd wash and dress in his suite and then maybe, since he wasn't going to bed anytime soon, find Alice.

Gavin caught the gesture. "Got a late date with the anti-Jenna?" he called.

"You know I can't date a guest."

"Ah, the sweet irony of life."

Kyle was not amused. He would be the laughing-stock of his staff if he broke the very rules he'd laid down. Then there was the job review, his coveted pro-motion to corporate. Everything he valued, hanging in the balance.

Because of one beguiling woman. One amazing kiss.

"What the hell," Gavin said. "Maybe the taboo is what you like about her."

It's not.

"'Cause, gotta tell you, guy, I'm not seeing it."

Kyle was momentarily flummoxed. Then he remem-bered. "You know what? That's exactly what I said when you told me Melina was the one."

"Wait a minute." Gavin stood and tossed his smelly sneakers into the locker. The basketball rolled off the bench and toward the shower stalls. "You can't mean this Alice chick is the type of woman you'd fall in love with."

"Of course not." Kyle kicked the ball away. *I don't have the time or inclination for that, but if I did, she wouldn't be the* type. *She'd be the* one.

He looked at his watch once more. The hour hand was directly on eleven. Fifty-eight hours.

Maybe he did have the time.

The inclination would require more reflection.

Beat the heat! The new multimillion-dollar water park at the Prince Montez Oasis Resort features a wave pool and river canal, with slides and pools for every age group.

July 30
Dear Dylan,
Your auntie is having loads of fun in Arizona. But

it's hot! I'm brown (and red) from hanging out at the water park whenever I'm not biking, hiking or otherwise risking life and limb. How's your summer going? Has your dad taken you clamming yet?
XOXO,
Aunt Alice

The banded gecko is a familiar denizen of the Sonoran Desert. The nocturnal lizard is 4-6 inches long.

July 30
Hey, Danny!
Since you love tide pool creepy-crawlies so much, I thought you'd like this card. There are supposed to be lots of exotic animals in the desert, but I haven't run into them. They're smart enough to only come out at night. But the coyotes sure do howl! I'm going to the desert museum one of these days and I'll bring you back a souvenir.
XOXO,
Aunt Alice

Spring wildflower season in the Sonoran desert is a spectacular sight. Here, a yellow blanket of brittlebush covers a hillside.

July 30
Dearest Dody,
Five more days and I'll be back! I missed Arizona wildflower season, so you'll have to take me to Whitlock's Arrow when I get home. Pull out Grandma's old picnic hamper, okay? I'll have lots

of stories to tell, about meeting a cowboy, riding a horse and getting caught in a monsoon. I miss you and your brothers bunches!

Hugs and kisses,

Aunt Alice

A GROUP OF CELEBRANTS had spilled out of the doors at Hoodoo. Their voices carried on the night air to Alice as she watched from her vantage point on the elevated terrace outside the Manzanita Lounge. The celebrants faded into the darkness, but laughter and catcalls marked their progress. Soon headlights appeared in the night as the group drove from the parking lot onto the curving road between the palms.

"Hiya, Alice. You don't look like you're enjoying yourself." Chloe stood beside the table, holding a margarita glass half-filled with a lime-green concoction.

"No, I am," Alice said quickly, lightly. Chloe had been so solicitous, Alice didn't want to give the impression that she wasn't satisfied with her stay. "I'm just not up to dancing tonight. All that energy…" She waved toward the club. "Mine's spent."

"I hope that means your day went well."

"It did, except for my sunburn." Alice motioned for Chloe to sit. The terrace tables were filled now that the heat had broken.

"Doesn't look too bad." Chloe took a chair. "Slather on the aloe and you'll be fine." She glanced longingly toward the nightclub while picking grains of salt from the rim of her glass. "Are you sure you don't want to go dancing?"

"Not tonight."

"Too sore?"

Alice allowed herself a groan. Then a slump. "All

these sports activities are catching up with me. I can hardly move."

Chloe reached for her evening bag. "I'll schedule you for a massage at the spa tomorrow. In fact, it looks like you deserve an entire day of pampering." She pecked notes into her PDA. "What's your preference? Hot stone, Swedish or shiatsu?"

"I have no idea. I've never had a massage."

"Never? Wow, you're in for a treat. What about a brown-sugar-scrub facial? Or a body wrap—they do a mesquite clay wrap with warm jojoba body butter that's out of this world."

Alice touched her cheek, remembering how Kyle had held her face in his hands when they'd kissed. He hadn't seemed to mind that she'd been coated in sand. "I could use one, I guess. But can you make the appointments before noon? The rest of my day is already promised."

Chloe's eyes lit up. "Ooh, to whom?"

"The Cocktail Shakers. The St. Gregorys, Harrie, Mary Grace—that group. We're going boating. I think it'll be fun. More relaxing, anyway, than another desert hike."

"Maybe they'll bring along a young person for you."

"Actually, uh, Harrie mentioned a nephew. And Mags said something about a grandson, but he could turn out to be anywhere from ten to forty."

Chloe chortled. "Blind-date boating! I love it." She drained her glass. "I've got to run. It's my first night off in a week and for once I get to have some fun, instead of scheduling it."

"Oh, I didn't realize you weren't working. I'm sorry to have kept you."

"Stop it." Chloe tipped up her chin, making her

dangle earrings shimmer in the fairy lights strung along the railing. "You're my pet project."

Alice smiled, though her enthusiasm had waxed and waned. Particularly with the Jarreau brothers, she'd been distracted from her goal for the trip. "I have to confess—I spent the entire day at the pool, writing postcards to my niece and nephews in between dips."

"There's no need to feel guilty. The heat is draining even when you're acclimated." Chloe instructed Alice to check her messages in the morning for her appointment times, then set off in the direction of the nightclub.

Alice sat unmoving for several minutes, watching the palms sway. *Priorities. Keep your priorities.*

She snatched her handbag off the back of the chair and took out the list she'd written on her first evening at the resort. Many of her subsequent experiences weren't on it. *Good.* Her life on Osprey Island hadn't allowed for much spontaneity. Every trip away from home had to be carefully planned, especially doctor appointments for her mother. Ferry schedules, mainland transportation, frequent rest stops.

To be young and free again was a wonderful thing. She had to do it right, which did not mean fretting over a man. Either man.

She stood and went directly to the desk in the lobby. "Hi. I want to… I'm not sure how this works, but how do I call someone here at the hotel?"

"Another guest, ma'am?" the young male clerk asked.

"Um, no. Someone on staff."

"I see. Is there something I might help you with?"

"No, thanks. It's personal. I mean, private."

"You may use the house phone, but I'll need a name

or an extension number. And since it's after hours, you'll most likely get voice mail."

Alice hesitated. Maybe this wasn't a good idea. "You know," she said, "it might be better if I wait until morning."

There she went, equivocating again.

"On second thought." She squared her shoulders. A simple phone call was no big deal. "The name is Jarreau."

SHE GOT, as predicted, voice mail. The desk clerk moved off to help another guest, but his head still seemed cocked in Alice's direction.

"Hello." She cupped the receiver. "This is Alice. I hope it's okay that I'm calling. I just wanted to—" deep breath "—wanted to say that I'd like to see you again. Maybe you're avoiding me, I don't know. Maybe that's the way it has to be. If that's how it is and you're staying away on purpose, I, uh, understand. I guess. I don't want to cause trouble. But I wish...no, I *want,* if it's possible, to see you again. I'm only here for five more days. It wouldn't be so terrible, would it, if we got to be friends?" Her eyes veered to the clerk. Busy. "But I wouldn't say no to something—"

Beep. The voice mail cut off.

"More," she whispered into the dead phone.

"ALICE," KYLE CALLED.

She was standing at the front desk, her head bowed over the phone. A short conversation, but intimate, from her body language. She didn't hear him.

She replaced the receiver but didn't let go. The clerk finished with late-arriving guests and came over to where Alice stood. He said something Kyle couldn't hear and a look of surprise crossed the clerk's face, but he picked up the phone and punched a couple of buttons for her. Then moved off with seeming reluctance.

Strange reaction.

Alice's second conversation was even shorter. She wasn't calling home; the desk clerk wouldn't have to dial for her. Therefore, it was reasonable to assume she'd called someone in the hotel. Reasonable, also, to deduce that she'd called either him or Denver, rather than any friends she might have made—she'd likely have their direct lines.

The blood rising into his face didn't feel reasonable.

She turned, smoothing down her skirt as her glance slid past him.

"Alice," he said, stepping forward even though he was in his workout clothes, a sweat-soaked towel draped around his neck. "Over here."

She spotted him, way off in the corner. Her head poked forward like a turtle's. "Kyle? What are you—"

He met her halfway. "Excuse my appearance. I've been working out." He took her by the elbow to the staff door. "Come with me."

She hung back. "Where are we going?"

"Up to my suite."

"Your suite? But you didn't even get my—" Her mouth clamped shut.

"Get what?"

She shook her head.

"Don't look so alarmed." They passed through the corridor and got on the service elevator. He pressed the button for the penthouse floor, remembering how wowed he'd been the first dozen or so times he'd done that. Now all that mattered was the next rung up the ladder.

Nothing wrong with ambition, he thought, but his heart wasn't in it, not when Alice was staring up at him with her big brown eyes.

"I only want to talk to you," he explained, "but I'd rather not hang out in the lobby in shorts."

"I see." She still seemed uncomfortable.

"I'm not asking you up to see my etchings."

"Oh, well." She summoned a smile. "Too bad. I've always wondered what etchings looked like."

They'd arrived. He led the way along the empty hallway to his door, glad for once that the hotel wasn't fully booked. It gave them a semblance of privacy.

"Here we are." They entered his chic sitting room, furnished in subdued grays, tans and walnut brown. "Do you mind waiting while I take a shower?" He pushed aside the louvered doors of the kitchenette. "May I offer you a glass of wine?"

"Sparkling water, please."

He filled a glass with ice cubes and opened a bottle of Perrier.

She walked around the room, hesitating by his desk before moving on. She stopped to gaze at a large abstract painting that evoked a desert sunset. "This artwork is lovely."

He explained that the penthouse suites were hung with originals from several well-known Southwestern artists, then handed her the glass. "Make yourself comfortable. I'll be five minutes."

This wasn't the first time he'd had a woman up to his suite, but it was the first time he'd felt so damned nervous about it. Every word out of his mouth sounded completely lame.

The ice rattled. Alice hurriedly took a sip. "No rush.

I've got nowhere… I mean, I'm fine." She dropped onto the couch. "I can wait."

Maybe he wasn't the only one feeling inept.

AS SOON AS Kyle had disappeared into the next room and Alice heard the shower come on, she bolted over to the telephone on the desk. The message light blinked incessantly.

That rambling, uncertain message! The idea of him listening to it in her presence made her cringe.

Too late. I'm here now.

She took a moment, staring absently around the suite. It was done up in high-style hotel, with dark wood and a nubby almond-colored rug. The curtains had a bold geometric pattern. Everything in its place. But something wasn't right.

Then she realized what. There were almost no personal possessions. A few books on a shelf, but no photographs. One newspaper on the coffee table, still folded.

She slid open a desk drawer. Pens, pencils, paper clips, rubber bands, stamps, arranged in a teak tray. A sheaf of Oasis stationery and envelopes. A checkbook. The only item out of the ordinary was a green plastic frog on a key chain.

Where was all his *stuff?*

She returned to the couch, knotting her hands. She unknotted them, leaned back against the cushions and tried to relax. That was almost impossible. She hadn't dreaded a conversation so much since she'd met with Stewart to give back his engagement ring. Then, she'd been hurt, humiliated…pretty well destroyed.

In her perfect version of that meeting, Stewart would have gone back to his new fiancée with a black eye. Or at least had a drink dumped over his head. But in reality, she'd cried. He'd hugged her and patted her shoulder, said she'd find someone else.

Alice tilted her head back, breathing through her nose. To find, one must seek. She hadn't wanted to. Instead, she'd buried herself away on Osprey Island, the most familiar and comforting place in the world.

Sounds came from the bedroom. A door shutting, a drawer opening. Maybe he had a closet jam-packed with junk, but she doubted it.

Alice sat forward. *After six years, you damn well better be ready to seek.*

She put on a bright expression to greet Kyle as he walked into the room. "You look refreshed," she said. His damp hair was attractively disheveled. He wore a white polo shirt untucked over a pair of faded jeans. Bare feet. Very sexy.

"I feel good," he said, getting a drink for himself. "Working out is my release after a long day."

"I usually watch Johnny Depp movies."

He dropped ice cubes into a tumbler. "You like pirates?"

"Yes, but *Benny and Joon* is my favorite."

Kyle walked toward her, his feet silent on the rug. "I don't know that one."

She knew she had to speak, but her mouth seemed to be full of rocks. She swallowed. "Um, Kyle. I should probably tell you—"

"Hold that thought. I just need to check my messages." He picked up the phone, pressed a button and started to say, "In case of any emergencies," before he stopped to smile. "You left me one."

At least that had pleased him. She watched his face

while he listened, unable to look away, even when his eyes darkened and his expression became serious.

"Well." He put down the phone. "Looks like we're on the same track."

"We are?"

"I was going to come and find you, but then I saw you in the lobby."

"Why?"

"I was on my way up from the… Oh. You mean why did I want to find you?"

Her hands wanted to fiddle. She folded them in her lap. *Composure,* she told herself. *This* conversation, she'd be the cool one. "Yes. I think we need to lay our cards on the table, as they say."

Kyle sat in a chair across from her, slumped low with his long legs sprawled out. He grazed a knuckle under his chin. "This isn't about gambling."

"It's not? I beg to differ."

He slitted his eyes.

"The risk's not mine," she said, intending to refer only to the hotel fraternization code. But as soon as the words were out, she saw that she was also taking a risk. Somehow, without her knowing it, her heart, which Stewart had broken, had healed. Finally, she dared offer it to another man.

Sort of. Her departure date was still her safety hatch.

"You're, uh, the one with rules to follow," she concluded.

Kyle nodded. "It's worse than you know. I have a performance review coming up next week. A team from PM headquarters is arriving to evaluate the resort and the job I've done as manager. If the report is excellent, I'll be promoted to executive VP at corporate headquarters."

"Oh. My."

"So, you see, I can't afford a single misstep."

She frowned. "And I'd be a misstep."

"Not necessarily."

"I don't see how not."

"If we're friends."

"Of course. Just friends."

"Like your message said."

Good. Let's ignore that last part, just as we're ignoring our very un-friend-like kiss.

"Yes, my message." She lowered her eyes, then spoke so quickly her voice came out raw. "Did you hear the whole thing?"

Kyle tipped his glass from side to side, watching the liquid slosh. "You were cut off."

"Yes, well, what I was about to say was that I wouldn't mind being more than friends." She met his gaze. "We could have a romance. Or should I say, an affair. A short-term affair." Now that was what was called laying her cards on the table, even though her cheeks were burning with embarrassment. "No one would have to know. It could be a secret. Like our kiss."

His hand tightened on the tumbler. She thought the glass might break, but he reached forward and set it on the coffee table. His eyes never left hers. "That's a bold offer."

She matched his restraint. "That's a noncommittal response."

His chuckle rasped. "Yes, isn't it? I'm not sure what to say."

"You must have had offers before."

"Yeah, but not from…" He waved a hand at her.

Her temper flared. "My type."

"You're not my *usual* type."

"That's unfortunate," she said, still treading carefully. But what for? If she was going to do this, she really had to go for it.

She lifted her chin. "Because you are *my* type."

Kyle leaned forward. "What do you mean?"

How could he be so constrained when she was telling him that she wanted him? Did he not care? The humiliation of that made her think of Stewart. "You remind me of my ex-fiancé."

He frowned. "That doesn't sound flattering."

"Well, he was ambitious, too. I don't mind ambition, if it doesn't take over every aspect of a person's life." She stared. "Has yours?"

"Do you really care?"

"Of course I care."

"Then why offer me an affair?"

She looked away.

"A short-term affair," he added, deliberately repeating her words.

She cleared her throat. "I thought that's all you're interested in."

He nodded. "Maybe so. From my *usual* type."

"Oh, yeah? It's so different with me? Because I'm—I'm—"

The phone rang, mercifully preventing her from continuing.

"You've become someone special to me, Alice," Kyle said as he went to answer the phone. "Don't sell yourself short." He picked up, but concluded the call with a quick, "Yes, thanks."

He turned slowly, his expression thoughtful. "I'm sorry, but I have to go. There's a large group arriving—

magazine editors, a photographer. They're staging a photo shoot at the resort. I've got to greet them."

"Yes. I understand." Alice edged toward the door. "No problem. I'll go." Part of her wanted to run. Another part of her was frustrated by the interruption. She needed to know, for good or bad, what Kyle thought about her. The comment about her being "special" to him wasn't enough. It sounded too much like there should be a *but* after it.

A *but* followed by a *goodbye*.

Except…there was still the way he'd kissed her during the monsoon. That kiss hadn't been a goodbye. It'd been a hello.

"Please wait," he said, getting his shoes. "I'll walk you down."

"It's all right if you're seen with me?"

"It's fine."

"They know at the front desk that I called you."

"Right." Kyle frowned as he came back into the room. He'd put on a navy blue sports coat, too, and suddenly seemed more like the Mr. Jarreau she'd first met. "Wait'll the grapevine gets a hold of that."

"Oh, dear."

"Never mind. It'll give them a distraction."

"The thing is…" she began as he ushered her out the door. Whether it was his reassumed professionalism or the fact that she was ashamed of her behavior, especially the impulsive come-on, she was beginning to think she'd made a grave mistake.

After ringing for the elevator, Kyle turned to look at her. She had to finish.

"The thing is," she said, "I also called Denver."

CHAPTER NINE

THE ELEVATOR RIDE was tense. Kyle was silent until they'd reached the lobby. Only then did he say, in a tightly wound voice, "Why did you call Denver? Did you leave him the same message?"

Despite the hotel's air-conditioning, nervous humidity rose off Alice's skin. She might look guilty, she might feel guilty, but she was innocent. Practically. "It's not what you think," she said as the doors slid open.

"When it comes to my brother, it's usually worse than I think." Kyle put out a flat palm, standing aside for her to get off first. Controlled and gentlemanly above all.

She didn't budge. "But this is me."

His expression was remote. "How well do I know you?"

"Better than that, I hope."

"If you'd run into Denver, instead of me, would he be getting lucky right now?"

"No! I did call him to, well, accept his invitation to the moonlight trail ride. But it wasn't going to be a date. It's a group thing. He only asked me because he's supposed to."

Kyle snorted. "Right." He took her by the arm, his fingers like a vise, and escorted her from the elevator. "If I got first dibs, that means my brother was the back-up date." He shook his head. "I don't know what you see in him."

"It's never occurred to you that there might be some ways you two are alike?"

"Hell, no."

"Two sides of the same coin. There's something intriguing about Denver's attitude. Devil-may-care. I've never been that way."

"Yeah? Trust me, you'd have a different opinion if you experienced the lifestyle up close."

"That may be. But I'd like the chance to find out on my own." That didn't come out the way she meant it. Her attraction to Denver was about taking a short walk on the wild side. There were no romantic intentions. But he was fascinating.

Like Kyle.

He was giving her a long measuring look. She was certain she hadn't met his standards. He stepped away. "Good luck, then."

"Wait," she said.

Across the lobby, a woman called, "Kyle Jarreau!"

He swung away from Alice to greet the Amazon charging toward him. "Bettina Brown."

They exchanged a brisk hug. "It's Mrs. Probst now, off the job. I married Emery."

"At last."

"We did it in Vegas with an Elvis impersonator officiating. Delightfully tacky." The woman was nearly Kyle's height and weight, dressed in jeans and a dashiki with chunky Navajo jewelry. Her eyeglass frames were Donna Karan. "*Extremely* impolitic for the magazine. But I just couldn't face the thought of what twenty yards of silk organza would do to my body. Come meet the gang."

Kyle hung back. "First, let me introduce you two. Alice, this is Bettina Brown, managing editor of *Southwest Bride.* They frequently stage photo shoots at the resort."

"Only because you're so adorable," the woman said, looking as if she'd like to pinch Kyle's cheek.

He smiled fondly. "Bettina, Alice Potter. She's a guest here."

"Oh. A guest." Bettina looked Alice up and down. "I was hoping she was a girlfriend, but I should have known—"

"Known what?" Alice had discovered that blurting out the thoughts she'd normally kept to herself often produced interesting results. Also humiliating. But she no longer cared.

The editor laughed gaily. "This fella, he's a slippery one." She patted Kyle's chest. "Just ask Jenna."

"She's here?" he asked warily.

"Afraid so."

"Great. Thanks a lot."

"You're both adults. Deal with it." Bettina pulled Kyle along. "Now come with me and say hello to the crew like a good boy before the entire lot of them are quaffing beer in the bar."

Alice hovered nearby, even though Kyle appeared to have forgotten her again. Blurting might serve its purposes, but being invisible was also beneficial. She'd learned many of the facts of life by hovering. The truth about Santa Claus. Her mother's early diagnosis, which she'd tried to keep secret. How her students, with the wit of ten-year-olds, had called her Miss Potty. That Stewart hadn't always been researching at the library like he said.

The *Southwest Bride* contingent included a number

of scruffy people, several suit wearers and half a dozen models. The models were easy to spot. They seemed twice as tall and twice as skinny as everyone else. Their dress varied from jeans and T-shirts to one sleek platinum blonde's tight black skirt and a camisole that exposed clavicles sharp enough to slice a tin can.

She, of course, turned out to be Jenna. Alice could tell by the way she looked at Kyle when he wasn't looking at her. Her demeanor was elegant but offputting, at least to Alice, especially after she overheard the model requesting blackout blinds, a dozen Diptyque candles and a bee-pollen shake to be sent to her room immediately.

If that's the kind of woman he prefers, I've got my answer.

Alice walked away, sure that no one would notice her leave. Or care. She felt indulgently maudlin.

Kyle caught her at the door. "Wait a minute. I'm sorry about that. They're important clients. We don't get many large parties booking rooms in the off-season. Accommodating them is paramount."

"You don't have to explain. It's your job."

He stood at the top of the steps with his hands in his pockets. A soft breeze blew along the front of the building, stirring the palms. "You're not like other women, are you?"

Was she supposed to agree? "I suppose I'm not." She nodded toward the lobby. "Compared with them."

"It's a compliment."

"I'm sure."

"You're unpretentious. You don't do the passive-aggressive thing."

"Like Jenna?" Alice's mouth tasted like foil. "You

were involved with her, right? So you must have some appreciation for her behavior. Or did you just put up with it in exchange for smoking-hot arm candy?" She didn't know how she managed to sound angry and discouraged at the same time.

"Jenna's not as bad as that. She's actually pretty easy to get along with."

"Wonderful. Then it must have been your other women you were comparing me with."

"Isn't your moonlight trail ride the same thing?" Kyle glanced at the doorman. "Erase that. Let's not go over it again."

Alice went down the steps. Now she knew, without a doubt. She didn't measure up. Again.

"Fine, if you'll do me a favor," she said. "Erase everything I said tonight. *Everything.*"

Kyle had followed her. "Does that include your date with Denver?"

"Ah, yes, Denver." She tried to act like she cared, that she was cavalier enough to keep two men on a string. "I don't know why I didn't see it right off. I'm unpretentious Alice. Cowboys are more my speed."

"That's not what I meant."

"I'm sorry. I don't usually get angry like this. I'm on holiday. I should be having fun."

"Yes, you should. That's what I want for you, Alice. I just can't give it to you." He cleared his throat. "Not personally."

She smiled blindingly. "Never mind. I have other plans."

"Don't do it, Alice," Kyle called after her. "He's not the man for you."

She knew that, but there wasn't enough money in the

world to pay her to admit it. Kyle might not see it, but she did: of the two brothers, Denver was her safer bet. With him, she was risking nothing.

Too bad safety was no longer her preferred choice.

THE GROUP HAD scattered by the time Kyle returned to the lobby. He stopped and spoke briefly with the new concierge, who'd done the check-in with impressive efficiency. Tomorrow there'd be an employee assigned to coordinate and facilitate the shoot. From previous experience, Kyle knew that anything could—and probably would—happen when it came to a bunch of creative professionals, but he was satisfied that the staff was as prepared as possible.

All that should have soothed him.

It didn't of course, and he knew why. The thing with Alice.

Alice and *Denver.*

She'd left so quickly that he hadn't had a chance to work on damage control. *If* that was what he wanted. There'd been a moment when tossing aside everything he'd worked for up to now had seemed possible. Logically, objectively, he knew the smart choice would be to leave things as they were.

Which left him unsettled, but at a standstill.

He stared at the elevator, his mind going back and forth with the opening and closing doors. The buttons lit, then blinked out. Up. Down. A simple choice.

Jenna glided over to him. Quite an accomplishment in three-inch heels that made them the same height. "What's wrong with you, Kyle?" She pouted. "You didn't even say hello."

"There wasn't a chance. You were avoiding me." He

looked directly into her eyes and felt nothing. He only hoped their breakup would continue as their relationship had: with no complications. "Hello. It's nice to see you again. You're looking well."

"How formal we are," she murmured. The elevator opened and she stepped inside, giving him one of her sultry smiles. "Going up?"

He could have made some excuse, but there was no reason for it. He stepped in.

After a short silence, Jenna shivered. "Brr. This place is an icebox."

She was the type to use that to her advantage, curling up to a man, batting her big eyes and stroking the guy's ego for taking such good care of her. In truth, she was no airhead; she managed her own stock portfolio and had plotted her career years in advance, preparing for the day she'd be too old to model. She claimed to be twenty-six. He'd always thought she was thirty at least. For a time, her poise and intelligence had made up for her lack of warmth.

He gave her his sports coat and she made a small purring sound as she slipped it around her shoulders. "You were always thoughtful, I'll give you that. There are times I wonder why I let you go."

They'd let each other go. Business trips and conflicting schedules had become more important than making time for each other. "We drifted apart," he said.

Jenna lifted her shoulders beneath the coat. "If that's what you want to call it."

"What do *you* call it?" He honestly wanted to know. He was curious.

"My God, Kyle. You're positively oblivious." She laughed without much humor, and her eyes glittered.

"You still don't realize that if you'd shown even the tiniest inclination toward a commitment, I would have been willing."

He couldn't say anything. Not once had he picked up those signals from her. "But you never…"

The elevator arrived at the third floor. Jenna gave him her patrician profile. "I don't chase men. They chase me." She got out. She wore an expression she'd never shown before—regret. Possibly even vulnerability.

He held the door, speechless.

"You never chased me," she said, almost as forlorn as Alice had sounded out on the steps. "I was barely a part of your life. I never met your family. You always held me at arm's length." Her expression hardened. "And so I decided I deserved better."

"You do," he agreed, feeling guilty for the first time over his lack of generosity. He hadn't even realized she wanted any of those things. "I've always wished you nothing but happiness."

That was the wrong thing to say. "Did you even notice when I was no longer around?" she asked, the words laced with anger.

"Sure I did." After about three weeks.

Jenna stared at him. "What about Miss Muffet in the lobby? Does she knew how fast you'll drop her?" Her lips twitched. "Maybe I should do her a favor and seduce you away."

Kyle was astonished. Had this entire conversation been about rekindling their romance? "Spite doesn't look good on you, Jenna."

"Spite? I'd call it a kindness." She walked away, her hips swaying. "If the mood strikes, I'm in 327."

The woman was as mockingly, aggravatingly attractive as ever, but Kyle was no longer interested. The elevator doors shut to the firm "no, thank you" in his head.

He let out a short laugh. What was wrong with this picture? Two propositions in one night and he was going to his suite alone. Gavin would call him an idiot. And he would be right.

IT WASN'T ONLY the hikes and rides that took it out of you, Alice reflected as she reached the condo door. She hadn't accounted for the psychological toll of change. Or the frustration of taking two steps forward and one step back.

The sight of a bunch of flowers on her doorstep swept the gloom out of her like a clean fresh wind. She smiled as she picked them up. Lavender, poppies, desert marigold, sunflowers—a random assortment with no nod to color or form. They'd been stuck into a plastic cup with an inch of yellowish water she suspected was melted ice. But the inelegance of the presentation did not erase the charm.

A note had been left under the cup, written on the back of a gas receipt. But not really a note at all, just a short lyric from the song "Go Ask Alice." What a goofball.

No signature, either, but she knew the flowers were from Denver. She couldn't tell if he'd got her message or not, the one saying she'd go on the trail ride but only as a PM guest. With Denver, that might not even matter. He was as easygoing as his brother was rigid.

She reconsidered. Neither was offering more than a temporary flirtation. That shouldn't be a disappointment when she was lucky to have the attention of even one man.

Choose Denver and the rest of her vacation would be a breeze, aside from the fact that he might lose his job.

Choose Denver, and Kyle would be permanently crossed off the list. If he wasn't already.

Alice sighed.

Choose Denver and she'd go home with pleasant memories of a few laughs, a few kisses, the ego boost of a sexy cowboy's flattery and attention.

Choose Denver and she'd never know if there might have been something real with Kyle.

THE NEXT NIGHT, as Alice was dining at the Roadrunner Café, Rivka came from the kitchen to present a special dessert—a rustic-pear tart drizzled with Riesling syrup. "This is a thank-you for helping us with the wedding cake," the pastry chef said. "You saved our butts—twice. Once with the cake and once with Mr. Jarreau."

Something of an overstatement, but Alice appreciated the thought. "You don't owe me a thing. But since it looks delicious, I'm glad you thought you did."

Rivka winked behind her round, wire-frame glasses. "It never hurts to stay on the good side of the boss. You seem to have influence with him."

Alice blushed. "Oh, no, really I don't."

This wasn't good. Kyle would not like to hear that the staff had noticed his interest in her. He'd withdraw even more.

"He's only being nice to me," she insisted.

Rivka departed. Alice slowly ate the dessert, reliving her day so that she wouldn't think about Kyle. It had been a long one, and unexpectedly strenuous. The condo crew had taken her to Lake Pleasant, where the St. Gregorys moored their motorboat. She'd returned hours later, stuffed with grilled burgers and fruit salad, dead tired from the effort to learn waterski-ing, her sunburn another degree hotter. A nap and a cold shower had revived her enough to come to the hotel for a light dinner.

She signed the bill and walked through the lobby, looking unobtrusively for Kyle. No sign of him. A pair of women with deep tans and big diamonds loudly dis-cussed the photo shoot going on at the grotto. "Wedding dresses, in this heat. Can you imagine? Just like that real bride earlier."

Alice had never watched a photo shoot. She walked around the main hotel, past the luxury *casitas* in lemon, strawberry and lime, each with its own small pool bordered by thick acacia and oleander hedges for privacy.

The grotto was at the edge of the massive water park, in a quiet area overhung by willows. She sat on a bench, well out of the way of the crew from *Southwest Bride*.

The normal nighttime illumination of the sixteen-foot waterfall and series of gladed pools was artfully subdued. The crew had set up bright lights on standards. The photographer, a short, wiry black woman in a tank and running shorts, alternated between looking into her camera and ordering the assistants from place to place to adjust the lights.

A makeup and wardrobe tent had been established off to one side. After the set had been pronounced ready, the models appeared, each in a different style of wed-ding dress. They came one by one out of the tent, attended by helpers who lifted their trains, dabbed their brows, smoothed their hair.

"Beautiful," Alice said, thinking she was alone. "Like swans."

"Do you think so?"

She jumped. "Kyle! I didn't see you."

He circled the bench. "I've learned to stay out of the way of these things."

"Why?"

"You see beauty. I see disaster. What do you want to bet that in about five minutes someone will have the bright idea to perch one of the models on the rocks? The slippery, mossy rocks."

Sure enough, the models were being arranged around the grotto-like living statuary. Jenna Malloy was the centerpiece of the scene, tall, slim and pale in a column of white lace.

Alice didn't feel envious. Only hopeless. "She's stunning. I can see why you went for her."

"It wasn't only her looks." He sat. "We were similar in many ways. We had the same lifestyle, the same sort of ambition. Neither of us was interested in marriage."

"Sounds ideal. What happened?"

"I didn't love her."

"Does that mean…" Alice bent her head. "No, never mind."

"Go ahead. Say it. Your observations are always illuminating."

"I was going to ask, seeing how alike you two were, if that meant that you don't love yourself, either."

He was quiet. She watched as the photographer, finally satisfied, began to take photos. She stopped for minor adjustments, a camera change, then started again. The models were asked to pose differently, which required another round of fussing.

"Was that too personal?" Alice finally asked.

"No, I'm thinking." Kyle had his elbows on his knees. He swung his head around to look at her. "It's not a question I've ever considered. Do you? Love yourself?"

She smiled abashedly. "I don't suppose I ask myself that, either. But maybe that's what this trip is about. Loving myself, for a change. Or trying to."

"You should treat yourself very well." He took her hand. Squeezed it. "You deserve it."

"I'm not some kind of saint or…or martyr because I devoted myself to my sick mother." She pulled her hand away. "I did what almost anyone would do for someone they love."

"You left your own life behind. That's admirable. I couldn't do—I *didn't* do that."

"My ambition doesn't run as strong as yours." *Or Jenna's, Miss Perfect Match. Except,* she reminded herself, feeling her hopes rise like a helium balloon, *he didn't love her.*

"Wait. What do you mean, you didn't do that?"

Kyle gave a small grunt. "Just that I've had opportunities to put my family before my career and I didn't. I always thought that giving them money and other kinds of assistance was enough to show that I cared."

"You gave your brother a job."

"I expect I'll end up firing him, too."

"Well," Alice drew out the word and they smiled at each other, agreeing before she finished, "he'll probably have done something that deserves it."

Kyle sobered. "Like dating you?"

"The trail ride is scheduled for my last night here. Would you fire him for that?"

"I'd be jealous of him for that."

"I'm having a hard time believing you. There's Jenna—" she pointed at the model, who was returning to the tent for a wardrobe change "—and there's me. We're not anything alike." Same claim he'd made about Denver. But *she* was right.

"I told you," he said. "I wasn't in love with her."

Alice was having a hard time catching her breath. "Last night. You said—"

"I didn't get to say enough." Her hand was on the bench and this time he didn't merely hold it. He stroked it, threading and unthreading their fingers. "I'm trying to work it out, Alice. Us. I like spending time with you, and I want to do more of it, but with my position here, that's difficult."

"I do understand. Really." She gulped. "I'm not being sarcastic the way I was last night."

"It's okay."

"I have to tell you—Denver's not really any competition. I like him, he's fun to be around, but there's nothing there. The message I left him was not the same message I left you, even if it was accepting a so-called date."

"That's a relief. Except I should have figured that out myself, knowing you."

She lifted her head. "You said that you *don't* know me."

"What I meant was that I don't know *enough* of you."

"Same here." Crazy, intoxicating hope fluttered in her throat. "How do we change that? *Can* we change that?"

"Sunday," he said abruptly. "I'm going away for the day."

"Oh." She counted the days remaining of her vacation. There weren't enough.

"Would you come with me?"

Her eyes widened.

"I'm stretching the rules," he acknowledged. "But look at it this way—when I'm away from the job, I'm my own man, on my own time. I can share my time with anyone I want."

"You'd have lots to say if one of your employees tried that line."

"We'll consider it a friendly outing. Nothing romantic intended."

"Mmm." He must have seen her disappointment.

He turned her hand over, touched their palms. "There may be more truth to that than I'd like. I have a…it's a kind of obligation, I guess you'd say. I hadn't intended to go at all, but someone said something that hit home. About…about the way I don't let anyone into my life."

Alice's interest was piqued. He didn't often stumble over his tongue like that.

"We'd be going to visit my family," he continued. "It's my mother's birthday. I haven't seen her in quite a while."

Nothing, not even an invitation to the No Tell Motel, could have surprised her more. "And you want to take *me?* To meet your *family?*" That was a big deal where she came from.

"It's not as much about that as it is a way for us to get to know each other. They live in Nevada. It's a two- or three-hour drive. Plus, if anyone asks, a family birthday party is a damn good cover, especially considering my family." He gave her a slightly lopsided grin, but she could see his nervousness. He was letting her in.

Alice tried to think the invitation through, but there was something wrong with her brain. She couldn't hold on to a single thought except that Kyle was not aloof, he was not uninterested. He truly liked her.

He studied the activity by the waterfall. "You'll learn a lot about me there. More than I might want you to know."

The models were back, freshly coiffed and gowned.

Alice scarcely noticed. A cool mist had lifted off the lagoon. It felt delicious, but a longing for the fresh breezes of Osprey Island came over her. Home was easy, familiar. Safe.

Not like this strange place with its searing heat and jagged rock. And men like Denver and Kyle, one so fast and the other already more important to her than she was prepared for.

Prepared?

For once, she would *not* prepare.

"That sounds fine to me," she said, wanting to touch him but aware that someone might see. She leaned, pressing her shoulder to his. "Sunday, then. It's a non-date."

CHAPTER TEN

"His name was Henry Humbert," Alice said a few minutes later, entertaining Kyle with stories of the day's outing with the Cocktail Shakers. "But he told me to call him Hank. He's Harriet's nephew."

"Clearly, that family has a thing for alliteration."

"The man was not a Hank. But he was a Humbert."

"No sparks?"

"Not even a flicker. He might have been fifty-five, under the toupée. I don't know what Harrie was thinking."

"I'll have to send her a thank-you note."

Kyle liked the way Alice blushed.

"Then there was the St. Gregorys' grandson," she said. "Colton. Whew, he was handsome. Tall, well built, with teeth so big and white you could have watched movies on them. He used enough product in his hair to fill an oil tanker. He taught me to waterski."

"Hmm." Kyle abruptly decided that he didn't care to talk about other men.

"You're red," he said, grazing a hand across her shoulders. They had moved to stand on the bridge that overlooked the waterfall, still watching the photo shoot, which had moved to a backdrop of sago palms. The models stood around looking bored while Jenna posed with flowers in her hair.

"My sunblock wasn't as waterproof as it claimed." Alice wiggled her shoulders. "Your old girlfriend is staring at us. Have you ever waterskied?"

"Yes, and I've surfed, too. I once held a position at a PM hotel in San Diego."

"You're lucky to have a job that takes you all over the country."

"It's been an experience."

"I always thought I'd travel during my summers off. Except that most teachers end up taking a second job, and then comes marriage and children, and before you know it you're thinking about retirement accounts, instead of expeditions to Machu Picchu."

"Do you want children?"

"Yes." No hesitation there.

"With Colton St. Gregory?"

"Ha. I must have forgotten to mention that he's ten years younger than me." She looked up at Kyle. "And you? Any ambition to have children?"

"We'll see. The right woman has to come along first."

"Yeah, you men," she teased. "You all have plenty of time."

"I'm getting up there. Thirty-six."

"Positively ancient." She pretended to stagger before gripping the arched railing. Blue-green water swirled beneath them, propelled by hidden jets. "Are you a *wunderkind,* or what? To be manager of a huge resort like this before age forty seems an impressive feat."

"I'm exceptionally dedicated."

"I suppose that's what it takes." Now she sounded dubious. He usually had no trouble impressing women. "Do you ever think about easing up on yourself?"

"Maybe after the next promotion."

"Or the next."

She cocked her head to one side. She had a way of appraising him that was a bit unsettling. He was never quite certain what she saw, especially since she'd admitted comparing him to her ex-fiancé.

He wanted to win.

But it wasn't a game.

"Tell me about your family," she said.

"Sunday's soon enough for that." The decision to go to the party, not to mention asking Alice along, was a big step for him. If she knew what she was in for, she might back out. And he really wanted her to come.

Alice's gaze slid toward the models. "Your girlfriend's finally gone."

He didn't look. "She's not my girlfriend."

"Not anymore."

"She never was, really. We weren't…like that."

"Like what?"

"In love."

"Have you ever been?"

"Sort of." He'd loved, but never all the way in love.

"Then the answer is no."

She was right. He'd just felt too chagrined to admit that he'd never been willing to fall in love. "You have, huh."

"Yes, with Stewart," she said with a frown. "There's a temptation to say it wasn't really love because of the way it ended. But that's revisionist history. I did love him. Maybe it wouldn't have lasted for the long haul, but at the time he seemed like the man for me." She turned her head, and the ends of her hair brushed over the pink skin on her shoulders and neck. "Who's to know?"

He pushed away from the railing. "I would want to be certain. To *know*, without a single doubt."

"Yeah, well, when you come up with a way to guarantee a relationship, clue me in."

"Don't worry, I will."

She looked quickly at him. "You sound like a man on a mission."

"I wouldn't say it's a mission. But I am taking a look at where I want to go from here." He turned toward her, unable to resist touching her hair. With her, he wasn't in control, and he was starting to realize that was what he needed. Lani would have laughed at him and said she'd told him so.

"The view in this direction is very nice," he whispered.

The smallest smile turned up the corners of Alice's mouth. Her eyes drew him in. She was reaching up to put her hands on his chest when someone called to them.

"Hey, you two on the bridge! You're in our shot."

They jumped apart. The models had been repositioned while he and Alice were talking, putting the two of them directly into the picture.

"No!" a second person yelled. "Don't move. You're perfect. Stay where you are." The photographer. She held a finger up to keep them in place while gesticulating for an assistant to give her a handheld camera.

Her authority kept even Kyle from disobeying, but he protested. "I can't be in your photos."

The models turned. They'd been lined up along the bank so that the bridge was behind them, with the waterfall cascading beyond. Jenna, holding a massive bouquet made up of sprays of orchids, seemed amused by Kyle's inadvertent participation. She smirked.

Bettina Brown came to stand on the bank of the lagoon. She planted her hands on her hips and gave Kyle a stern look. "Don't be a stick in the mud. You're only background for the shot. You'll be an unidentifiable blur." She twirled her fingers. "Look at each other the way you were before. Get closer. That's right. Put your hands on her waist. Lean in. You're young and in love and you're making us a very pretty picture, thank you very much."

Kyle followed the editor's instructions. The mood wasn't quite the same, but Alice still had the liquid eyes and the tentative smile. He bobbed his head. "Do you mind?"

"Not at all. I never thought I'd be a model, even if it is only as background scenery." Her eyes went to the real models. Jenna was no longer all that amused. "This is fun."

"Watch out. They might put you in a wedding dress."

"That'd be new. The first time, I never got the chance to try any on." She wrinkled her nose. "Not that I'm saying this is the second time, but it may be as close as I come to participating in a wedding party."

"Not likely." He pressed his fingers against the thin cotton of her dress, almost no barrier at all to the warmth of her skin beneath it. Above his thumbs, her rib cage expanded. "You'll be a sweet bride."

Her breathing hiccupped. "Maybe." She looked away.

Lucky guy, Kyle thought automatically, before he remembered that he didn't believe in luck. But what would he call it, having Alice stumble into his path?

Fate? He didn't believe in that, either.

"Love it!" called the photographer. "Jenna, give me serene, instead of ticked off. You're a bride, not a wife."

Bettina barked out a laugh.

Kyle and Alice locked eyes. "Is this okay?" she asked softly. "I wouldn't want you to get fired for posing with me."

He winked. "That's not going to happen."

"When the case goes to court, they might use the photos as evidence."

He leaned in even closer. Yes, there was a definite glint of mischief in her dark eyes. "Oh, yeah? Evidence of what?"

"Of our..."

Their...?

"Our illicit flirtation."

"You over there, yoo-hoo!" someone called. "Lovers on the bridge."

"That's us," Kyle said.

Neither of them turned.

"We need a kiss," the voice said. Probably the photographer.

"Yes! Yes!" That was Bettina. "Give us a kissie, Kyle."

"I only kiss one woman at a time," he said, though only Alice could hear.

"I'm conservative that way, too." He felt the warm whisper of her breath on his chin.

"Too conservative to kiss me in front of an audience?"

Her head moved an inch. "Who, them?"

"Nobody." He lowered his mouth to touch hers. "There's nobody but us."

She stretched up on her toes and he tightened his hands around her waist and just like that they were alone, despite the onlookers and the corporate rules and the rivalry with his brother. Their kiss was not deep except in feeling, but that was entirely new for Kyle. If he'd been a reflective man, he might have recognized right then that he'd fallen in love.

He did know something had happened—something special.

"Hold it," called the photographer.

They didn't listen. Alice sank down on her heels again. He pulled back, enough to see that the light shining from her face had nothing to do with the photographer's equipment.

She smiled. "I wonder if I can get a copy of that photo."

"No need. I'll be glad to recreate the moment anytime you like."

Prince Montez Oasis Resort is a popular location for weddings and receptions. Here, a bride and groom pose on the Moonlight Bridge overlooking the grotto waterfall.

July 31
Dear Sue,
My vacation is going so fast! You won't believe the wonders I've seen and the adventures I've had, including posing for the camera during a *Southwest Bride* photo shoot. Okay, I was only background, but still—who'da thunk it?! I also tried fishing and waterskiing. Tomorrow it's a trip to a birthday party. More on that when I get home. I've met the nicest people.
See ya,
Alice

BY SUNDAY, Kyle was king of the world. The resort was running like a well-oiled machine, as it should, since he'd been oiling the machine for the past three years. He wondered briefly if he *should* take the day off, even so, but he'd already promised his mother and sister. Or at least Lani had for him. They also knew that he was bringing a guest.

Sweet naive Alice. She didn't know what she was getting into.

It ought to be an interesting day. Lani had said that his family sounded excited and happy on the phone. He hoped they were.

He was going to try his best not to keep his emotional distance. Alice would see that he wasn't as closed off and rule-bound as she believed.

He got his own car from the parking facility rather than the company car, then washed the clean windows and shined the hubcaps while waiting for the air-conditioning to cool the interior. He repositioned the floor mat. He adjusted the passenger seat.

Driving up to the condos, he had an urge to tap the horn to announce his arrival. His father had done that. Long blasts as whatever run-down vehicle he'd been driving at the time rattled up the dusty road to their house. Kyle and his brother and sister would fly home from all directions. Their mother, if she wasn't working, would bang open the screen door and stand with one hip cocked, unmoved until her wayward hubby gave the high sign: windfall or bust.

Eventually Kyle had stopped waiting for his dad. He'd made up his mind that his only way out was on his own. But the rest of them were either more stubborn or more hopeful. He never could decide.

A distressed Alice opened the door to his knock. "I don't know if I should go with you," she said, holding her arm in front of her at an awkward angle. "I went on the early-bird mountain bike ride and I had a run-in with a cactus."

He took her arm. The skin was red and tender.

She winced. "Careful. It's sore. The bike guide pulled

the needles out and dosed me with ibuprofen, but it still hurts." She brushed at her straight white skirt. "My leg, too."

Kyle looked closely. "There are still some tiny pieces of cactus in you. We need some glue."

"What for? I don't have any glue."

"Let me see." He went into her kitchen, a sleek galley-style with dark cabinets and granite counters. A small cooler sat open on one. She'd been packing drinks and snacks. He opened drawers until he found one with the accumulation of flotsam that even vacationers collect. A few tools, menus from the resort restaurants, extra batteries and a full bottle of Elmer's Glue.

"Sit down," he told Alice, crossing to the bathroom for a warm washcloth. She sat, her face pinched.

"Nothing to it," he soothed, returning to sit beside her. He put a rolled-up towel beneath her arm and squeezed a large dollop of glue over the infected area.

She let out a squeak. "What in the *world?*"

"Hold this for me." He gave her the washcloth. "You'll see." He spread the glue over her arm with his fingertips. "This is an old trick."

There were red prickles on her calf, leading up beneath the three-inch slit cut into the hem of her skirt. He touched her knee. "May I?"

She inhaled. "I can do it."

"No, don't move your arm. Let the glue dry." He slipped his hand under the skirt and pushed it higher up her thigh. "Can you elevate your, uh, leg?"

She put the affected leg on top of the other. "I'm sorry to be a bother."

"No bother." He smoothed the glue liberally along her calf and over the outside of her thigh. Her leg wasn't tight and muscular, but it had some firmness to it. And a very nice shape.

He coughed. "You should see a doctor for antibiotics."

"The glue treatment isn't a miracle cure?" Her voice was high and light with a bit of a wobble. "You know what works best. My mother said it, and I bet yours did, too."

She was looking at him expectantly. "I don't… What?" he said.

"A kiss. A kiss makes it better." She put her hand on his, which he hadn't moved from her thigh. "Didn't your mother tell you that?"

"That's not her style."

Alice blinked. "Is it really gauche of me to ask for a kiss at this time of the morning?"

"I think—" he shifted closer "—any time is appropriate."

They kissed. For longer than Kyle had intended. Her lips had a way of making him lose track of things, of rules and plans, even of goals. Previously that would've made him crazy, but now he was learning to like the feeling of freedom.

He eased away by trailing his mouth across her cheek, along the line of her neck, where he breathed her scent, as sunny and clean as the outdoors. "I can't move," he said against her skin.

She moaned. "Me, neither."

"For real. My hand is glued to your thigh."

"Oh!" She twisted against him. Her thigh flexed beneath his palm, lifting her skirt.

He peeled his hand away. "Ahem. My couchside manner needs some work."

"I don't know about that." Alice's face was flushed, but she was smiling. "I feel a lot better."

He rubbed his thumb over the glue that had dried on her arm. "Now we peel this off and—see?—any of the plant matter still in your arm comes with it." He lifted grayish shreds of the stuff off her arm, cleaning up the rest with a warm washcloth. Then he went to work on her leg.

"I feel like a snake shedding its skin." She put her hand in her lap to hold the skirt in place.

His gaze veered away. "There." One last wipe of the cloth over her thigh. "Finished. Does that feel any better?"

"Um, maybe." She closed her eyes. "Yes, I think it does."

"Still, we should pop into the doctor's office before we leave. If you're up to the drive, that is."

"Where are we going again?"

"A small town called Elk River. My sister moved there about a year ago. Maybe you should stay—"

"No, I want to come along. I'm looking forward to meeting this mysterious family of yours. You haven't even mentioned their names."

"Daisy is my sister and Luanne is my mother," he said, wondering if bringing Alice home with him was a good idea. For more than twenty years, he'd been cut off from his family, emotionally at first, and then physically, too, when he'd earned a scholarship and went away to school. They hadn't understood his drive. He hadn't understood their willingness to accept the status quo without a fight.

Until Alice, none of the women he'd dated had expressed any particular interest in where he'd come from. Not even Jenna, he'd thought. Maybe he just hadn't picked up on their signals because it was easier that way.

Keeping himself at a distance from his family's chaos had been his only chance to better himself. Now that he'd achieved his goals—or almost—he could afford to let them back in his life.

Knowing how they felt about him, what his sister might say to turn Alice away, Kyle was aware that he could be making a huge mistake.

DENVER JOGGED UP as they were preparing to leave. Alice had never seen him move faster than a stroll, but there he was, sweating and panting beneath his straw cowboy hat.

He yanked the hat off and whipped his head like a wet dog. Alice was given a friendly nod; Kyle got a narrow look. "Thought you were gonna leave without me, man?"

Kyle put the cooler in the backseat. "How did you know…?"

"I was invited." Denver smirked. "This guy," he said to Alice. "He kinda forgets I'm his brother."

"You have your own car."

"It's not as fine as this one." Denver swept a hand over the midnight-blue chassis of the Cadillac roadster. He opened the door and tossed his hat onto the front seat, then leaned over to study the interior. "The old man always wanted a Caddy. Never did get one, s'far as I know."

"Fingerprints," Kyle snapped.

Denver lifted his hand off the window. "Fussy," he said, adding to Alice, "I used to wrinkle his bedspread just to bug him."

"Let's go." Kyle came around the car to hold the door for Alice. He handed Denver his hat. "If you're coming with us, you're riding in the back."

"Yessir, boss."

"And cut that out. We're not on the job today."

Denver winked at Alice. "I should sa-a-ay not."

Kyle was tight-lipped as they drove away from the resort. Alice snapped on her seat belt, catching Denver's eye over her shoulder. He'd sprawled out across the backseat, his thumbs hooked in his jeans, hands framing the large silver rodeo buckle. The sleeves had been torn off the worn plaid cotton shirt he wore half-unbuttoned. His grin was as cocky as ever.

"So what's goin' on here?" he asked lazily. "You two hooking up or what?"

Kyle's eyes went to the rearview mirror. "Stay out of it, Denver."

His brother laughed. "Caught you red-handed."

"She's with me as a friend."

Alice marveled at Kyle's authority. Even she, minutes from a thorough good-morning kiss, believed him.

"Well, then, you got Mom and Daisy all excited for nothin'."

"How do you mean?"

"Mom called me last night, said you were bringing a girlfriend home after all these years. You must be ready to make an announcement, she said. That was when I knew I had to come along."

Kyle muttered under his breath. They were on the freeway now, heading west. The heat seemed to rise in waves off the blacktop. Like the steam coming out of Kyle's ears, Alice thought, as he said tightly, "I don't know where she got that idea."

Denver poked his head between the seats. "Damn confusing, ain't it? You got any idea what would have given the old lady that impression, Allie?"

"None at all." She became self-conscious of her primping. A manicure and pedicure at the spa had seemed reasonable after the hot, dirty bike ride. But then Mags and Mary Grace had come over and insisted on fixing Alice's hair in a French twist that had seemed a good idea at the time. With her hair up, wearing her best pearl-teardrop earrings was necessary. And then the sandals with heels, because of her skirt.

"Like Kyle said, I'm just a friend."

Denver hummed appreciatively. "A mighty purty friend."

"Don't talk that way," Kyle said.

"You jealous?"

"That's not—" He bit off the retort. "Why do you enjoy sounding like a corn-pone yokel?"

"Just being me." Denver settled back. "Can you say the same?"

"I'm not faking it. I got myself an education. I've worked damn hard not to be like—" Kyle cut himself off again. He breathed through his nose.

"Sorry," he said quietly to Alice. "This isn't happening the way I'd hoped it would."

"Don't worry," she said. "Relax. Things don't have to be perfect for *my* benefit."

"Man, I gotta get me some o' that education," Denver said from the backseat.

Alice twisted around. "Don't be a brat, okay?"

"I'll have to turn this car around," Kyle put in, straining for the humor, but at least willing to make the attempt. She smiled at him.

"Truce?" Alice asked Denver.

"Whatever you say, ma'am." He slumped lower and dropped the hat over his face. "Gonna catch me a few winks. Wake me when we get there."

She sat forward, exchanging a glance with Kyle.

"Family road trip," he said apologetically.

"It's okay. I've survived a few in my time." She and Jay, in the backseat, squabbling and elbowing each other. They'd never gone far. To Bangor for the fireworks. To Jonesport to visit their elderly aunts.

"I was practically raised in a car," Kyle said.

"You have just the one sister and brother?"

He nodded. "Unless my dad had a second family somewhere else. As often as he was gone, that wouldn't have been a shock. Except that he didn't even take care of the one he had."

"At least you must have been happier after you were settled in one place."

"It wasn't as bad."

But not good, she extrapolated. "My father was always nearby, running the boathouse at the marina. My mother could rarely get him off the island. I didn't find out until just a few years ago that she'd wanted to travel, but she gave that up for marriage and kids."

"Did she resent that?"

"She said no. But when her will was read…" Alice's eyes burned at the memory of what her mother had done for her. She pinched her thumb and index finger together. "She left me money. Not a lot, just what she'd been saving in dribs and drabs over the years. She gave instructions that I was not to use it for medical bills or putting a new roof on our cottage or anything practical."

Alice sighed, remembering Jay's confusion that the small legacy should be Alice's alone. She'd tried to explain, but her brother hadn't shared the heart-to-hearts she'd had with their mother. Those times had been worth the years of not having a life of her own.

"The money was for a trip," she continued. "Mom knew I wanted to travel, and she said in the will that now I'd be able to. I'd be doing it for both of us."

Kyle squeezed her hand. "And so you chose Arizona in July?"

She laughed. "That was me, trying to be frugal. I thought that if I did the vacation-house swap, I might be able to stretch my mother's money into several trips. No one told me just how hot it would be here." But even if she'd known, she would have come, anyway. Luxury in the desert was the total opposite of her humble cottage by the sea, and that was what she'd needed.

Denver spoke up from the back. "Bet your mom woulda wanted you to blow it all in one shot."

"That could be." Alice grinned at Kyle. "But I have no complaints about what I got."

Kyle glanced at her. "Even with all your misadventures?"

"Even with. Every sting and bump and bruise has been worth it." Until right then, she hadn't realized how true that was.

CHAPTER ELEVEN

DENVER LOUNGED against the outside wall of the gas station, his hat pulled low over his eyes, a water bottle in one hand. "I'd rather be having a beer," he said when Alice stopped beside him on her way back from the women's washroom. "But the boss would complain."

"It's barely noon."

"Yeah, and you're turning into a prig just like him."

She smoothed her skirt over her hips. "Why are you being so hard on him?"

Denver didn't answer. He took a long slug from the bottle. A droplet trickled along the stubble on his chin, but he didn't wipe it away.

She stared at his lips. He had full, sensual lips.

"Did you get my flowers?"

She blinked and grabbed a pair of sunglasses out of her bag. "I sure did, thank you. They were lovely. Did you…did you get my message?"

"Yep. You'll like the trail ride. The moon'll be full. I won't even hold you to that part about being a hotel guest."

"But I meant it. We can't be involved. For one thing, I won't be the reason you lose your job."

"Lose my… Well, now, that would be the height of hypocrisy, wouldn't it? Seems *the boss* doesn't care much about that 'no involvement' rule or you wouldn't be here. Anyway, jobs are easy to find." He pushed away from the building and looped his arm around her waist. "Gals as sweet as you aren't."

His breath tickled her ear. "Get away." She pushed him away, laughing.

He glanced at the car, where Kyle was filling up at the pump. "You know you want me," Denver whispered as she walked past. "My women always check out with a smile on their faces."

She stopped short. "How many have there been?"

"What the boss doesn't know…"

"I guess I can stop worrying about being the reason you lose your job. You'll handle that on your own."

Denver just laughed. "Your schoolteacher side is showing, sweetheart."

"If I could, I'd make you go stand in the corner." She smiled, finding it impossible to stay mad at the man. She'd dealt with her share of troublemakers before, but they'd mostly been ten years old.

Surprisingly, Denver sobered. He pointed the water bottle at Kyle. "I figure I'm just a blip on the radar. But what're you gonna do if you cost *him* a job?"

Even though the temperature had soared past 110, she got a chill. "How could that happen? He's in charge."

"There's always someone higher up the food chain. Kyle's bosses are coming in this week."

"He mentioned that, but surely they wouldn't fire him."

"You never know what that bunch of fat cats'll do. He's got the whole darn staff spit 'n polished, but that doesn't mean something still can't go wrong."

"Nothing will go wrong." She crossed her fingers. "You…you wouldn't cause trouble, would you?"

"For Kyle?" Denver shrugged. "I could care less if he gets his promotion."

"You couldn't."

"Huh?"

"You *couldn't* care less. And that's not kind. He is your brother."

"Yeah, well, there're things about him you don't know, Allie. He's not as perfect as you think."

She frowned. "I don't think he's perfect. He's human."

"Human?" Denver snorted. "My brother's the tin man."

Alice shook her head, perplexed.

"Let's get going," Kyle called, holding her door open. In jeans and T-shirt, he still looked serious and thoughtful. Was that because he'd seen her in conversation with his brother?

She murmured her thanks and slid into the Cadillac. Denver climbed into the back. While Kyle walked around, his brother reached out the open window and rapped his knuckles against the door.

Alice jumped.

"No heart," Denver said. "He's capable of cutting you out of his life just like that."

The car's interior was still cold from the air-conditioning. She was able to tell Kyle that was why she suddenly had goose bumps.

"Hey," Alice said twenty minutes later, "it's been nearly three hours of nothing but dirt, rocks and cacti. Are we almost there?"

"Almost." Kyle felt rather grim. They'd crossed the border ten miles back, and with every additional mile he grew more certain he'd made a mistake by bringing Alice to Elk River for the birthday party. Did he really want her to know him as well as she would after today? He'd thought he was taking an important step, one she'd appreciate. But as their arrival loomed closer, he'd become more worried about whether, at the end of the day, she would still like him.

He wasn't at his best around his family. They knew just where to find the sore spots.

"Ah, the old hometown," Denver said fondly. He'd never had a problem with their vagabond lifestyle. He'd been born knowing how to roll with the punches, whereas Kyle had never learned not to take life so seriously.

"What's it like?" Alice asked.

"We're not actually going to the original family home," Kyle said. "That was sold years ago."

"Sold," Denver echoed. "Yeah, sure. Why don'tcha tell it like it is?"

"I was being discreet."

"Here's the unvarnished truth, Allie," Denver drawled. "The old man lost the family estate in a poker game. But he forgot to tell his wife and kids. One day, the county sheriff showed up at our door with an eviction notice."

Alice looked at Kyle with large solemn eyes. "For real?"

Her sympathy made him uncomfortable. Sympathy was too close to pity. He didn't want either.

He nodded. "We had only a few days to pack and get out."

"That must have been hard."

"The place was a dump," Denver said, "and so was the town. I was glad to get away from there."

"How old were you, Kyle?"

"Fifteen." Although Kyle hadn't thought about the incident in years, the memory was still sharp.

The town was small; everyone had known they'd moved into the one-bedroom apartment of their mother's friend, also a waitress. At school, he'd acted as if he didn't care that he had to share a pull-out sofa with his eleven-year-old brother and wash dishes in the greasy spoon after school to help pay for the family's meals. He'd even kept quiet when the kids spread the rumor that the Jarreaus ate the leavings of the regular customers. Until Daisy, only eight, had cried at recess over being called Garbage Guts.

That was when he and Denver had teamed up and beaten the crap out of the instigators. They'd landed in the principal's office, branded as white trash in spite of Kyle's honor-roll status.

A few months later, their mother had found a new man, another wannabe high roller who'd claimed she'd earn big bucks in Vegas as a cocktail waitress. Kyle had been ready to move out of the family home by then, especially as he knew that Vegas, like most of his parents' big ideas, would be a bust.

"It was a long time ago," he said.

They were driving through the town now, passing the dinky post office, the run-down pharmacy, the school where all the grades fit into one small building. He turned off the main road before they reached Traveler's Rest, the diner and truck stop where his mother had worked.

"There's Jimmy K's old house," Denver said from the back.

Kyle glanced at a well-kept ranch with a wishing well in the yard. It looked almost the same. "And the Mabreys'."

Alice smiled at him. "Feeling nostalgic?"

"Maybe." Elk River was no place of consequence, but it was the only home they'd ever had, the only place they'd stayed long enough to make friends. It was familiar, even after twenty years. He'd figured that was why his sister had moved back—to give her children a taste of the same.

"Childhood memories are strong," Alice mused.

"They were for Daisy. She always talked about Elk River as if it were Shangri-la." That was as much as Kyle would admit. "It's her house we're going to. She lives with her kids and her second husband." A lout, in Kyle's opinion, but at least this husband was sticking around, unlike the first one.

"Nieces or nephews?"

"One of each."

"I've got three. I miss them." Alice glanced in back to include Denver. "You two must make great uncles."

"Denver, maybe. I don't visit that often." Kyle found Daisy's place and turned his car onto the long dirt driveway. Her house, a split-level stone-and-cedar ranch, was set back from the road. Cartoon-colored plastic toys pockmarked the seedy lawn.

"Let's roust the troops." Denver reached past Kyle and blasted the horn, three times in quick succession.

"It's a nice house," Alice said, looking through the windshield. "I like the roses." Rosebushes lined the driveway beside a split-rail fence. Climbing roses wove around the stair rail of the elevated entrance and deck.

"That's my mother's work," Kyle said. "She always said that someday she'd have a yard where she could plant roses. There's a mother-in-law apartment out back for her."

Two chubby children in swimsuits had burst out of the house, shouting excitedly. Denver got out and scooped them up in one big hug.

"That's Arabella and Jasper," Kyle said. "Denver's good with them." He shrugged. "I had trouble remembering how old they are until Lani put their birthdays on my electronic calendar."

Alice laid her hand on his arm. "It's going to be all right."

"Of course." He was more abrupt than he'd intended, jerking the key from the ignition.

She pulled back. "I thought you seemed apprehensive. Maybe I was wrong."

His mother and sister stood on the deck, looking down at his car.

"No, you're right," he told Alice. He'd better warn her. "There's friction between me and Daisy. So don't feel unwelcome if she seems irritable. It's not you, it's me." He paused. "But do me a favor and don't believe everything she says about me, okay?"

"Hey, I know how families are. There're usually hurt feelings and old grudges. They can be hard to let go."

"But you stayed close to your family." Daisy was moving down the steps with her hands on her hips. She was pregnant again. Her first with Judd, and she hadn't even bothered to tell her oldest brother. He supposed that was his fault, for shutting her out when the friction between them got too distracting.

"You're lucky," Kyle said to Alice. He rubbed his hands on his jeans before reaching for the door handle. "But then, I don't suppose you ever had to fire any of your family."

LUANNE "CALL ME LU" Jarreau looked Alice up and down while they shredded cabbage for the coleslaw. She yielded a butcher knife with the skill of an old pro.

Alice felt uncomfortable under the scrutiny. "I'm afraid I overdressed." She should have come in flip-flops and shorts, but Kyle had given her no clue of what to expect.

They were having a birthday lunch in an air-conditioned room at the back of the house. At the moment, Daisy's kids, plus a few neighborhood pals, were in the backyard, jumping between a wading pool and a water hose manned by Denver. Kyle and his sister were parked in a couple of lounge chairs. The husband, a trucker named Judd, had wandered off toward the big rig he kept parked in an adjacent empty lot.

"Are those real pearls?" Luanne rolled her cigarette to the other side of her mouth and peered at Alice's earrings without a break in her chopping. Sliced cabbage flew indiscriminately.

In fear for her fingers, Alice didn't dare scoop it up. "Handed down from my mother."

"I heard tell you lost her. That's a real shame."

"Thanks. Her name was Dorothy. She sent me on this vacation."

"From beyond the grave?" Lu let out a *hah!* that became a cough. Ash dropped from her cigarette. "My kids won't listen to me even while I'm alive and kicking."

"Not even on your birthday?"

"Nosiree. I'm sixty-five and I get no respect."

"Oh, I doubt that. Kyle seems to respect you. He told me that you worked very hard for a lot of years to keep the family together."

"Damn straight I did." Lu took the cigarette out of her mouth to exhale a stream of smoke, and Alice was finally able to scrape the mound of cabbage into a bowl. "Huh. He did finally agree to come to my party, but it took some persuading, lemme tell you."

"He's busy at work."

"Nothin' new 'bout that." With sure hands, Luanne twisted open a jar of salad dressing. She upended it over the bowl and slammed her hand on the bottom of the jar. "So you're staying at his hotel? Fancy place, eh?"

"I'm in one of the condos. But I've only got a few more days."

"You'd think he'd let his old ma come and stay, wouldn't you? But you'd be wrong."

Alice mixed the glop into the cabbage. "I'm sure he—"

"What're you, settin' your sights on him?" Lu shook her head. She was about five-seven, a few inches taller than Alice, and rawboned, with a hard stringy body that spoke of years spent working on her feet. Her hair was cut short and dyed red.

"That's not—"

"I'll share some advice, since you seem like a nice girl," Kyle's mother interrupted again. "Give him up now. Save yourself the heartache. That boy—*both* my boys—they're like their dad. Got their eyes on the prize."

"Oh."

Don't believe her, Kyle had said.

She was trying not to. But it was hard, especially after he'd pretty much admitted that he was planning to fire his brother.

"Now, that man, lemme tell ya, *he* was a handsome devil," Lu said with a sigh. "I knew there'd be no good end to our marriage, but I just couldn't help myself."

"I'm not sure…are you divorced from Kyle's father?"

"Nah. We're still legally wed, after all these years. But that doesn't amount to a hill of beans when the dickweed hasn't shown his face in more years'n little Jasper can count."

"I'm sorry."

Luanne grabbed the bowl and swept from the kitchen, Alice at her heels. "Like I always told my hubby when he showed up with his hat in hand, *sorry* doesn't pay the rent, but a twelve-hour shift slinging hash surely does." Her laugh carried like a foghorn. "Bring that platter of sandwiches, will ya, hon? We got a hungry crowd out here."

KYLE HAD BROUGHT the birthday cake in a bakery box with the PM logo, but it was Denver who carried it from the kitchen, candles ablaze. He sang with gusto.

The rest of the family joined in. Kyle stood, but Alice remained in her chair. Jasper, three years old and wearing a soggy pair of pull-up diapers beneath his swim trunks, had planted himself in her lap. It was like holding a sack of wet cement, but she was happy. She felt included.

She wished Kyle felt the same way. He was stiff. Uncommunicative. Not the thoughtful, wry and generous man she'd come to know, the one who was even willing to poke fun at himself. The tension between him and his sister was palpable. Alice didn't understand why.

Daisy was a plump strawberry-blond version of her mother. She had a blunt way of talking that veered toward harsh. The favor she showed Denver seemed designed to spite Kyle.

Alice didn't like her.

Daisy passed a wedge of cake to Alice. "You can feed Jasper. He's taken to you."

The little boy said "Yah!" and thrust a chubby hand into the frosting.

"Bad, Jas," Daisy said flatly. She handed a slab of

cake to Denver. "Here you go." Kyle got a narrow slice, pushed lazily across the table.

Alice wiped Jasper's hand with a paper napkin and gave him one of the plastic forks. "Do you know how to use a fork?"

"Yah!"

Arabella piped up with "How old are you, Grandma?" She was a chunky nine-year-old with big blue eyes and wispy hair the color of sand. She'd already asked Alice if she was going to marry her uncle Kyle and then said, "Why not? Because he's mean?" She'd offered Alice Denver, instead. Alice had politely declined, though she wondered what on earth Daisy had been saying around the girl. Kyle deserved a lot better.

"Sixty-five years young, pumpkin," said Luanne.

"Are you retired?" Alice asked.

"Sure am," Luanne said. "Kyle forced me to, couple years ago."

Her older son lifted a forkful of cake in an ironic salute. "Terrible of me, wasn't it?"

"No, that was sweet," Alice said after a silence. If they wouldn't defend him, she would. She was also fairly sure he was funding the retirement.

"My corns'll never heal," his mother said, "but my arthritis isn't so bad these days."

"Kyle said you're the gardener. I noticed the roses when we drove up. They're lovely."

"Lots of fuss and bother," said Daisy. "And Jas is always getting stuck with the thorns."

Lu snorted. "Grammy'll teach him to keep his hands where they don't belong." She ruffled the boy's hair. "My little monkey."

He'd stuffed half of a huge bite of cake in his mouth. The rest was on his face. "Yah, monkey!"

Alice reached for a clean napkin. She smiled at Daisy. "When's the next one due?"

"I'm six months."

"Do you know if it's a boy or girl?"

"We're gonna be surprised."

Judd, the silent husband, grunted. "Better be a boy."

Alice looked at Arabella. "Girls are just as nice."

"Right," Kyle said forcefully. "Two nieces for me would be twice as nice."

While her daughter beamed, Daisy frowned. "Like you'd ever see either of 'em."

"I'll try to do better. I'm sorry I haven't been around for so long. But you know how my job is."

"Yeah." She sneered. "I know how your job is."

"Children," snapped Luanne, "it's my birthday!"

Daisy's mouth was puckered into a knot. She narrowed her eyes and turned to Alice. "What would you say about a man who'd fire his own sister? His own sister who was a single mom with two kids to support. That's a really shitty thing to do, don'tcha think?"

Alice felt her mouth drop open. It was *Daisy* he'd fired! She'd thought he'd meant an impending dismissal of Denver.

She glanced at Kyle. His expression was stony but resigned, as if he'd heard this all before. Many times over.

"I...I guess I'd have to know the circumstances," she said.

Daisy sniffed. "There aren't any circumstances that justify it."

"I had no choice." Kyle's voice was toneless. "*You* gave me no choice, through your own actions."

"I told you. I didn't do it."

"Gawd, Daise," Judd suddenly erupted. He slammed his beer can on the table. "It's been more'n a year already. Give it up, will ya? The poor guy's paid his blood money."

"You never take my side." Daisy burst into tears. "And I'm *pregnant!*"

There was a dreadful silence around the table, filled only with Daisy's sobs. At least, Alice thought it was dreadful. She fumbled for something placating to say. "I'm sure that…that…"

"Never mind her." Luanne lit a cigarette. "It's hormones."

"Please don't fight," Arabella squeaked.

Kyle stood. He commanded attention. "I've got to cut this short," he said briskly. "I promised Alice a drive around the town." Without looking at her, he plucked Jasper out of her arms and set him on the floor. "Ready to go?"

She shot up. "Yes."

Arabella's face crumpled. "What about Grandma's presents?"

Kyle patted her head. "You go ahead and help her open them, honey."

"Hey, you abandoning me without a ride?" Denver was the only one at the table who seemed to find the family fireworks entertaining.

"We'll be back." Kyle looked as though that was the last thing he wanted.

"Go on, then." Daisy mopped her face with a paper napkin. "Get out. We'll do just fine without you and your friend."

"Gawd, Daise," Judd was repeating as Kyle and Alice hastily departed.

CHAPTER TWELVE

KYLE PULLED OFF the highway and parked at an empty stretch of land, staring at the scrub grass and creosote bushes. One lone cottonwood tree stood in the distance.

"It's gone," he said.

"Your old house," Alice guessed.

"Yeah." They got out of the car and walked. Took in the empty window frame with grass growing through the openings, a couple of leaning fence posts, sagging wire still attached, a rusty bucket half-filled with sand.

Kyle shaded his eyes. "I wonder when it was torn down. Daisy never mentioned it."

"Had to be quite a while ago." In the tall grass, Alice picked out the crumbling ruins of the foundation. "You never came by before?"

Kyle lifted a weathered board and a lizard scurried out from beneath it. "I never wanted to come back. Thought the place would bring up bad memories." He dropped the board. "But this is nothing. Just a lot of nothing."

She went over and hooked her arm through his. "You must have good memories here, too. Those aren't gone."

He made a noncommittal sound. "Daisy was Arabella's age when we left. A cute little thing. She really looked up to me then, her big brother. She loved me."

"She will again."

"I doubt that. She blames me for everything that's gone wrong in her life."

"Why? You gave her a job, didn't you?" Just like Denver.

"Right after I was promoted to manager at the Oasis. She worked as an office receptionist for nearly two years."

They picked their way through the scrub. He stopped and put his foot on a dusty pile of cinderblocks. "Here're the front steps. Would you like to sit?"

Alice hesitated. Kyle grabbed a bunch of pampas grass and used it like a broom to sweep away most of the dirt. He produced a handkerchief, spread it across the step and gestured her to sit.

"Thank you." She perched on the blocks. He *would* be the sort of a man who carried a clean hankie. "Your sister seems to think I'm something better than I really am."

"Forget it. Daisy has an inferiority complex, like my mother. They resent success."

"I don't see why."

He sat beside her, took a breath and put his head in his hands. He scuffed the dirt with his shoe. "Daisy wasn't always that way, only after things didn't work out for her with her first husband. She got bitter then." He rubbed his eyes before straightening and looking across the barren patch of land that had once been his front yard. "She hated working at the resort. Said it wasn't a real home."

"She was staying there with her kids?"

"Yes. We have employee day care. Jasper was a baby. Her husband had taken off while she was still pregnant. It didn't help that our mother was constantly chiming in with I-told-you-so."

"She had it rough," Alice conceded.

"I liked having them around. Arabella, especially. There were ponies in the stable. I used to take her there every chance I had. I guess her mom's turned the child against me since then."

"I knew you were a good uncle."

He frowned. "She's asked me to bring her back to the resort so she could see the water park. And I haven't found the time."

"Schedule it."

"Right."

"Like any other appointment." She brushed her fingers over his arm. It was brown and strong, with tiny hairs that looked gold in the sunshine. "You made time to come today."

"Mainly because of you." He turned his hand over.

She slid hers into it. "How so?"

"Hearing about the sacrifices you made for your mother got me thinking about why I've resented the things I've done for my family. I always thought I'd given them whatever they wanted. But I withheld myself." He laughed shortly. "I'm not sure they want me anymore, but I may as well try."

"It'll take a while to heal the hurt feelings. Yours, too." Alice turned over what he'd said. "But none of that is really because of me. It's all you. *You're* making the change."

"Yeah, well, I also thought you'd take me more seriously if I let you into my life."

"I *was* taking you seriously."

"Not that night when you came to my suite and said—"

She winced. "Let's forget that ever happened. I had vacation brain. I was trying to get your attention or something."

He chuckled and lifted her hand to his mouth. The kiss he pressed to her knuckles made her shiver in the heat. "You're too good for me."

"You know that's so far from the truth!" She yanked the pins from her hair and the French twist disintegrated into a hanging mess. She shook it out. "I'll never be as sophisticated as your old girlfriends."

"Do you think I want you to be?"

"Well, maybe." Her experience with Stewart and his replacement fiancée was coloring her response, but she couldn't help that. "Jenna is gorgeous."

"And we're not together." He brought both his hands to her head and smoothed her hair. "You have your own beauty. It's not fleeting. It's real."

He kissed her. She melted into his arms, amazed that a day that had turned so wrong could suddenly seem right again. Her lips parted and he licked into her mouth.

He pressed kisses along her throat. Her back arched, her breasts pressed against his chest. She let her head drop back into the cradle of his hands, losing herself in pleasure. Allowing it, at last.

The low rumble of thunder in the distance brought her back. "Tell me the rest of the story," she whispered into his ear after kissing it.

He moaned. "Now?"

"While I've got you distracted."

Kyle spoke swiftly. "I'd already put Daisy on notice after she was caught using an unoccupied hotel room for…*assignations* with another member of the staff."

He didn't give Alice a chance to comment on that astonishing news. "Next our office manager noticed that small amounts from petty cash were missing." His fingers were still laced in her hair and he pulled them out. "The manager started a private inventory and found other things disappearing, as well. Minor items like office supplies at first, but then an old answering machine. A few weeks later, a laser printer. Two of the secretaries had cash taken from their purses."

"Oh, no. It was Daisy?"

"We set up our own sting operation, with a hidden camera and a wallet and an expensive watch left in one of the desks. As soon as Daisy was alone in the office, she went for it."

"Ouch."

"Yeah. Ouch. My own sister."

"But how can she possibly blame you?"

"Easy. I set her up. I fired her. Even with the evidence on camera, she swore she was innocent, that she was only going to put the cash and watch away where they'd be safe." He snorted. "Like in her own bag."

"She should be grateful that you didn't call the police."

"I couldn't do that."

Alice mulled the sequence of events. They didn't quite add up. "How did she end up living in a nice house in Elk River? By marrying Judd?"

"No, he came later." Kyle seemed reluctant to explain. Finally he added, "She was going to be homeless after leaving the resort. What else could I do?"

"*You* bought her the house?"

He nodded. "She married Judd a few months after moving to Elk River. I don't know him well, but he seems like an okay guy. I'm hoping it'll work out."

Alice was angry, for Kyle's sake. "I'm sorry to say this, but your sister is a miserable ingrate. She treats you horribly, even after everything you've done for her." Alice got even angrier. "And now you've hired

Denver, too, who doesn't give you any more respect than Daisy."

"I told you—they resent me."

"While they leech off you."

"Family's family. I'll always help them out. You, of all people, know what that's like."

"I suppose." She leaned her chin on her fist. The air was growing heavy with humidity. A slight breeze rippled the long grass and she tilted her face toward it. "But they still ought to be grateful."

"It's all right. I got over expecting anything from them years ago."

She looked at him sideways. "How did you turn out the way you did, coming from the same home as your brother and sister?"

"Maybe because I was the oldest. I was thirteen when I made up my mind I wasn't going to live like that for the rest of my life. I knew I'd need a scholarship to get to college, so I concentrated on schoolwork above everything else. Every time we moved, I made damn sure my transcripts were in order and that I stayed caught up in my classes."

Alice blinked back tears before he saw them. "Good for you," she said around the lump in her throat.

He picked up her hand. "Yeah, but I'm starting to see that I've been too single-minded."

"That was the only way you could manage."

"Back then." He studied her with regret in his eyes. "It's different now. I'm already a success, even without the next promotion. I don't *have* to be so rigid anymore. But it's become a habit, I guess."

She lifted her face to the rising wind. The brilliant blue of the sky was graying at the edges. "I know all about the board review, or whatever it's called. I don't want to be a distraction."

"No worries. I'm set. I've been working on acing this presentation for weeks." He sounded confident. "Nothing can go wrong now."

That was what she'd said to Denver. No worries. She prayed that Kyle was right, knowing she'd been guilty of steering him wrong. She hadn't fully understood how cavalier she'd been—flirting with Denver, trying to entice Kyle into breaking the rules himself. She'd been reckless.

Reckless, but besotted.

"It's going to rain," he said, rising from the step as thunder crackled and boomed in the distance. He held out his hand to her. "We'd better go."

Lightning brightened the horizon, a split-second flash that lit the dark clouds.

Ominous. The hair at Alice's nape lifted. She took Kyle's hand.

THE STORM LASHED the windshield, but went eerily quiet the instant Kyle drove under the tiled roof that extended past the loggia to the parking area. Through the gray sheets of rain splashing down on the courtyard, squares of welcoming lamplight beamed from the condominium buildings.

"Door-to-door service," Kyle announced. He powered down his window before turning off the engine. The air in the car was heavy and damp. "You won't even get wet."

Alice had been quiet on the drive home. Even Denver had known when to shut up, except for his "See ya around, hypocrite," when they'd dropped him off at his quarters near the stable grounds.

It was early evening. They'd all made nice with each other after Kyle and Alice had returned to his sister's house. Daisy had accepted a hug. His mother had opened her birthday gifts, regaled Alice on the ins and outs of rose gardening, then lured them into several games of Bunco. Still, they'd left earlier than planned. He'd blamed the long drive ahead of them.

At her door, Alice said, "I'd offer you a drink, but I don't suppose you should come inside."

"Is that an invitation?"

She hesitated. "Yes, if it's all right."

"There are no resort police patrolling for staff law-breakers."

But as he spoke, a door opened farther along and a silver-haired woman poked her head out. "Oh, it's you, Alice. Hello. And Mr. Jarreau." A big smile. "Storm'll be stopping soon, wouldn't you say? There should be a fine sunset."

"That was Mary Grace," Alice said after the woman had gone back inside.

"One of the wedding crashers."

"They, uh, have been keeping an eye on me."

"Does she have a nephew, too?"

"A son. And he's a doctor. He lives halfway across the country, but Mary Grace is giving him my phone number." Alice opened the door. "If I'd known about the senior set's propensity for matchmaking, I'd've worked my mother's friends for dates."

"You don't want to marry a lobsterman."

"Why not?"

"Too much pinching." He goosed her and she shot into the apartment with a squeal of laughter. He followed, telling himself he'd only stay for a drink.

Alice went to stow the empty cooler in the kitchen. "Is wine okay? Or you could check out the bottles on the liquor cart. They came with the place. I'm not much of a drinker."

He chose a bottle of whiskey and polished a highball glass on his sleeve. "This place is nicely decorated."

"I lucked out," she agreed, coming into the living room with an ice tray and a glass of white wine for herself. "Even if every day has been hot enough to roast a Christmas turkey."

"The rain cools it off." The storm had ceased. He opened one of the glass sliders and a fresh breeze billowed through the stuffy room.

She'd dropped to the sofa. He watched while she kicked off her shoes. There was something sensual about the action. Perhaps her throaty moan as she wiggled her toes.

She swung her legs up. He sat on the other end of the sofa. "So there are strangers staying at your house on Osprey Island right now?"

"Yes. It's odd to think of it."

"Do you know anything about them?"

"It's a him. One man. All I know is that he's a police officer on vacation. He said he wanted solitude." She leaned back on the cushions and ran her hands through her hair. "I sent him a ferry schedule and left the house keys in the mailbox."

"That's trusting."

"I suppose I'm a trusting sort."

He lifted his glass, let the liquor coat his tongue before swallowing. "Do you trust me?"

She took her time answering. "That depends what you're asking of me."

"I'm not sure."

Her face was obscured by her tousled hair. "I'll know when you know."

"You trusted me today," he said, surprising himself.

"I did?"

"Daisy said some unkind things. Probably Denver has, too."

Alice looked away for a moment and he had a bad feeling. But then she brushed her hair back and met his eyes. "I see who you are. Even if they can't."

He rolled the glass between his palms. "I appreciate that."

"Families," she said with a chagrined smile. "They're complicated."

"Not what you bargained for on your vacation, hmm?"

"Truly? I didn't expect any of this." She sat forward, pulling her legs beneath her. "But I'm glad I found it. I wanted an experience."

His gut tightened. He put his drink down. "Cactus needles included. How's the arm?"

She extended it. "Feels good."

He ran his hand along the skin of her arm. Soft, smooth, pink and gold like the skin of a peach. "Yes, it does." His heart was a bass kettle drum. *Boom. Boom. Boom.* "And the leg?"

"You're just hoping to get your hand up my skirt."

He pretended shock. "Really, Miss Potter."

She laced her fingers over her eyes. "Did I say that?"

"Alice…" Her name was honey in his mouth. "We shouldn't."

"No, we shouldn't. Especially with your big day coming up."

"Why don't we forget about that for at least one night?"

"I can't. *You* can't."

"You're wrong." He yanked her into his arms, almost violent in his urgency to prove he was more than a businessman.

She was trembling, her eyes huge. Her lips soft.

"I can," he said, realizing that, indeed, he could. Far more easily than he'd expected.

Gulping she tried once more. "I don't want to get you into tr—" But he cut her short, his lips coming down hard on hers. The kiss deepened. Their bodies tangled as they found the right configuration—as if they'd been choreographed.

No. As if they'd been freed.

THE BEDROOM WAS completely dark when Alice opened her eyes. She felt Kyle beside her, exhilarated by his presence, comforted by his warmth. She listened to his breathing, wondering if he was as wide awake as she. It wasn't so late that they could sleep through the night.

If he stayed.

Beneath the sheet, he touched her hip. "We missed the sunset."

"There'll be another," she said. Then the realization that there might not be another sunset *for them* hit her hard.

"What?" he asked.

"Nothing."

He rolled onto his side, molding his body to hers. "Don't say *nothing*."

"Mmm. *Something*, then."

"Something sweet." She heard the smile in his voice.

"Something surprising."

"Something sexy."

"Something...singular."

They both went quiet.

"How do you mean that?" he asked cautiously after a moment.

"I go home in three days."

He didn't respond.

She pushed further. "You go back to work tomorrow."

He kissed her shoulder. "So?"

"We'll have to pretend this didn't happen."

"Don't say that. Not now."

That was what he said. What she heard was *"Not yet."*

She turned over to face him, but found she'd become shy and couldn't look directly into his eyes. She nuzzled against his chest. Began to pepper it with kisses.

With her eyelids closed, she wasn't shy. With her eyelids closed, she remembered every kiss and caress and surprised gasp of their lovemaking. Whenever she'd felt uncertain, he'd known exactly how to put her at ease. How to overwhelm her with kisses so that she wasn't thinking.

"I'm hungry," she said.

He chuckled. "So am I." He'd grown hard against her belly.

"There's not much in the kitchen, but I do have cheese and crackers and half a bag of trail mix."

"No cookies?"

"Macadamia nut." She felt herself blushing in the dark. "There's a spa in the private courtyard. We could be completely decadent and eat in the water, under the stars."

"Like this? Uh, nude?"

"Haven't you ever skinny-dipped?" She sprang from bed before she thought too much, aiming for the robe hanging on a hook on the bathroom door. "Meet you there in five."

"I'VE IMAGINED doing this since I first got here," she confessed, stretched out in the spa. "Look at those stars!"

"You could have asked Denver," he teased.

"Oh, I considered that."

"Did you really?"

The water bubbled around them. "Nope. Not *really*. But he's not shy about being available."

"Hmm."

"Don't put on the stern-boss face. That can't be news to you."

"I've looked the other way. After the disaster with Daisy, I didn't want to know what Denver might do."

"He's pretty open about it—playing the cowboy Romeo, that is."

"Right. It's all fun and games until he flirts with the wrong woman."

"Let it go, Kyle. He's okay. I know you two have your problems, but he's not mean, I don't think. Not vindictive."

"Like Daisy."

"Well…yeah."

"I'm sorry she was rude."

"That's not your apology to make."

"I feel responsible, though. Someone has to be."

She sighed. "I know."

"You, too?"

"Jay tried, he helped, but…" She turned in his arms and leaned her forehead against his jaw. "At some point, you're going to have to let go. You can't be responsible for them forever."

"You were, with your mom."

"That was different. Your family is capable of making it on their own. Your siblings, anyway."

"Don't worry. When Denver goes too far, that's it. He's done for."

"What if he surprises you?"

"I wouldn't count on that." Kyle toyed with a damp wisp of hair at the back of her neck. Finding his voice. "You, though. You, I can count on."

She hunched her shoulders.

"No?" he said.

"It's better not to make promises, don't you think?" she said softly. It hurt like a blow. "That is the way you want it, right?"

His heart pounded. "But I didn't expect that from you."

"I'm known for my practicality."

He felt heavy. *Singular.*

"I thought we weren't going there tonight."

"It's hard not to when you say...things like..." She was lolling, almost dozing off with her chin dipping into the water. "Say things like that to me."

His arm splashed down into the water. "I can't wait until you check out."

Her eyes popped open. "Kyle!"

"Because then you won't be my guest."

"Oh. *Ohhh.*"

He caught her mouth with a kiss. "Don't give me up so easily."

"Giving you up would never be easy."

Small comfort, but he'd take it for now.

ALICE AWOKE in the dark a second time, a bleak early-morning dark. She closed her eyes, knowing at once that she was alone in bed.

Would Kyle be in trouble for spending the night with her? She was afraid that in the light of morning he'd decided they'd made a mistake. Dreaded that he'd be right.

She rolled her face into the pillow. Damn it, anyway. She was weak for losing heart so soon.

Also, increasingly angry at Kyle for leaving.

She sat up. Of course, he had to go, to show some discretion. His car had been parked right outside. She shouldn't blame him.

But irrational or not, she did.

"It's a woman thing," she muttered. A catch phrase between her and Sue. If cell phone service wasn't so spotty on the island, she'd call Sue right then.

"Dear Sue," she said to the empty bedroom. "Last night I ordered in room service."

Bawdy, but indirect.

"Dear Sue. Mom may be rolling over in her grave, but wow, am I ever getting my money's worth."

Crass.

"Dear Sue. Remember that hot tub I mentioned?"

"What was that?" Kyle stood in the doorway, dressed in yesterday's clothes.

Alice yelped and yanked the sheet up to her chin.

"Sounded like you were having quite a conversation. I swear I heard 'hot tub.'"

"I was writing postcards."

"Where?"

"Imaginary postcards."

"About hot tubs?"

She smiled. "P.S. Glad you were there."

His grin was morning-after awkward. "Then you're not mad at me for taking off so early? I was going to leave you a note."

She swallowed. "Sure. No problem. I understand."

He stopped rubbing the back of his neck. "You do?"

She waved him off. "Go on."

"We could have dinner tonight. A late dinner. I've got a lot to get done today. The board members arrive tomorrow."

"Let's play it by ear, then."

He hesitated, half turned to leave. "Okay."

"Get," she said, sliding down in the bed. "I'm going back to sleep."

"Will you be around?"

"Today?" She yawned even though she was wide awake and taut as a violin string beneath the sheet. "I have to check with Chloe. She may have signed me up for cactus wrestling."

He came back into the bedroom. "That reminds me. If you show any sign of infection from the cactus needles, call the concierge for an appointment at our clinic."

"Mmm-hmm." She was infected all right—with him.

"I guess I'll go, then."

She lifted a finger. "Bye."

He went, but she didn't hear the door. Sounds came from the living room and then he was back once more. He flipped something onto the sheet. "Here."

She raised her head. "What is it?"

"A postcard."

A postcard? "Great. Thanks."

"I'm going now."

"Then *go* already. Sheesh."

He came back, swooping in with a kiss. "That's better."

Lots. And right when she was trying not to fall in love with him, too.

Finally she heard the door click behind him and she could exhale. She let her arms drop. She hadn't had that many boyfriends, but was there anything more awkward than saying "goodbye, call me later," to a first-time lover?

"Chalk up another one under 'Strange New Experiences,'" she said to the ceiling.

She lifted the postcard. It was one of the freebies from a stack that had been left in the desk, along with brochures and hotel stationery. The front showed a nighttime glamour shot of the resort, lit like a movie set.

He'd written on the back.

But only one word.

She had no idea how to take it.

The Prince Montez Oasis Resort, Phoenix, Arizona—the jewel of the Sonoran Desert.

Thanks,
K

CHAPTER THIRTEEN

By the thirteenth day of her vacation, Alice had learned to horseback ride and waterski. She had driven a Razor in the desert and ridden a bike up and down a red-rock canyon. She'd boogie-boarded and sung campfire songs. Made a wedding cake. Had a massage. Drunk beers with a cowboy. Posed as a background model.

And fallen in love.

Rashly, recklessly, nonsensically in love.

With a man who'd told her "Thanks."

"Thanks," she said, shading her eyes at the stable door. "Thanks a lot. I owe you one, kid."

At the other end of the stable aisle, a cowboy sprawled on a stack of hay bales was silhouetted against the brightly lit doorway. Set into the wall above the door, a giant electric fan swept air into the row of box stalls. Warm air, but at least it was moving.

Alice walked along the aisle, Denver's eyes on her. A couple of horses dozed in the heat, their heads hanging over the stall doors. She stopped once to tickle Loco's whiskered muzzle.

Denver wore jeans, boots and nothing else, the brim of his hat pulled low over his eyes. The rippled contours of his torso glinted with sweat and flecks of chaff. He could have posed for Mr. August in a beefcake calendar.

Whew. "It's hot in here," she said.

"Sure is."

"You're not busy."

"Nope. Pull up a seat." He saluted her with a can of beer. "Want a cold one?"

"Yeah, sure, why not?"

"Help yourself, sweetheart."

A sweating cooler sat on the patchy cement, packed with ice and the last two cans of a six-pack. She took one of them and sat on the edge of a bale of straw. "No trail riding today?"

"We had a few go out this morning, that's all."

She ran her fingers along the seam of her jeans. "I thought I could fit in one more ride before tomorrow night. The monsoon cooled things off."

He grinned crookedly. "You're acclimating if you believe that."

"Maybe so." Her blood must have thinned, too. It had been racing through her veins all day.

She knocked back a third of the can in one drink and then had to stifle a burp. "How about that ride?"

Denver just looked at her. "Does Kyle know you're hanging out with his no-account brother?"

"Don't call yourself that."

"I'm sure you've heard it from Kyle."

"We actually haven't talked about you that much."

"He doesn't go around slapping himself on the back for giving his jerk-off brother a job?"

"No, he doesn't."

"Seriously?"

"Seriously."

Denver scratched his ribs. "That's something."

Something selfless.

He winked beneath his hat brim. "I'll betcha he'll have more to say when you'n'me go for that long romantic ride across the desert under the full moon."

"I thought it was a group ride."

"Doesn't have to be. In Westerns, schoolmarms fall for the cowboy, not the prosperous town merchant."

She shook her head, aware of the flush moving into her cheeks. "There won't be any of that. This school-marm is taking the next stagecoach out."

He chuckled.

She put her beer on the floor and got up to peek into the nearby stalls. Empty. Not much distraction there. She hadn't come to flirt with Denver. But she'd felt some sort of urge. Could've been one last chance to enhance her experience, but more likely it was to try to make things right between the brothers. She was still a helpmate, after all.

Denver climbed to his feet and stretched, every move fluid but slow, as if he'd been dipped in warm molasses. She watched out of the corner of her eye as he got a saddle blanket, then a saddle. The smell of leather and horse and clean straw was comforting.

He paused beside her, holding the saddle against his hip. "Who're you choosin' to ride?"

Her face burned. Did *everything* Denver said have to sound so suggestive? Was he doing it just to torment her?

She licked her lips. "Loco."

He upended the saddle on the floor. Came up close to her with his hand at the small of her back. His voice was low and intimate. "Are you *loco* for my brother? Or do I still have a chance with you, darlin'?"

"Oh, Denver. You know I'm not your type. Why cause trouble?"

"Who says you're not my type? Kyle?"

"He wouldn't do that."

"The hell he wouldn't. The day after I took you out, he sent around a memo reminding employees of the company's anti-fraternization policy." Denver moved closer. "Now, why'd he do that, d'ya think?"

She pressed against the stall boards. "I didn't realize…"

"He can't stand to lose." His hand was on her shoulder now as he turned her to face him. "My brother knows that romancin' the ladies is one area I've got him beat."

"I wouldn't be so sure."

Denver's expression hardened.

She kept her arms crossed between them. "I would like to know—what did you mean, about Kyle cutting people out of his life?" *Me,* she thought, although the way Denver had said it made her wonder how he'd been affected in the past. "You said he has no heart."

"You know what I meant, Allie. I can see it in your eyes. You're as wary of him as a mouse with a rattlesnake."

"You're comparing your brother to a rattlesnake?"

"Why the hell not? He's harmless most of the time, but you get too close and he'll strike fast."

"That's absurd."

"Ask Daisy."

"Kyle told me about that. Daisy was stealing. She deserved what she got."

"Did he tell you why she was stealing?"

Alice shook her head.

"It was our dad. He was in jail in Mexico over some damn business venture. He needed bail. And there was my brother with all the cash in the world and he wouldn't help."

"Kyle said he hasn't seen his father in years."

"Of course he hasn't. He refuses to."

She turned that over in her mind. "He must have his reasons."

"The old man's no saint, yeah. But I'm telling you—Kyle's cold." Before she could absorb that, Denver had shoved his hat to the back of his head and leaned into her, caging her shoulders between his arms. His face was so close to hers she smelled the beer on his breath. "You need someone warm, Allie."

"Kyle's been—"

Denver grazed his lips across her turned cheek. "Kiss me, darlin'. I'm so hot for you I'm burnin' up."

He was hot. Suffocatingly hot, parching all the air in her lungs. Her voice choked in her throat. She put her hands against his chest to push him away.

"That's it," he said, and brought his lips down on hers.

The kiss was electrifying, but not in a good way. The shock of having another man touch her the way Kyle had… She pushed him—hard.

Denver fell back, his arms pinwheeling and his face flashing his surprise.

Alice gaped. She wasn't *that* strong.

Then she saw Kyle.

WHEN HE'D WALKED into the stable and seen his brother putting the moves on Alice, Kyle had had every intention of holding his temper and delivering the usual lecture, even knowing that Denver wouldn't listen to a word of it.

But then Denver had kissed her, and the blood had roared in Kyle's ears. He'd reacted out of instinct. The kind of instinct he'd thought his long practice of discipline had overcome.

One yank of his brother's shoulder had pulled him

off Alice and sent him reeling into the stable aisle. That wasn't enough. Even though Kyle had caught a glimpse of Alice's shock, he couldn't stop.

He went after his brother, swinging wildly. The first blow landed in Denver's gut, a second caught him under the jaw. Denver's hat flew off. His teeth clacked together and his lip bled.

Kyle froze. In slow motion, he saw Denver coming at him, his face twisted in a snarl. Alice had clapped her hands over her mouth.

His brother's fist smashed into his face.

Kyle's head snapped back. Pain exploded in his skull. He heard Denver swearing, his own ragged panting, felt sweat stinging his eyes, blurring his vision. The leaden heat. The sharp tang of the stable.

He whipped a hand across his face as Denver staggered toward him.

Kyle's fists bulged.

"No!" Alice put out her arms.

She caught him in a tangle. "No more fighting."

Denver shouldered in. "I can take him."

"Stop it!" She held them apart with a hand on each man's chest. "You're fighting for nothing."

"Nothing," Kyle repeated.

"If you think—" She broke off to drag in a breath. "What you saw…that was nothing."

"Bullshit." Denver jutted out his jaw. "She liked it."

Recognizing the bravado as so much bluster, Kyle bit down on his rage. He yanked at his tie and collar to loosen them. The damn things were choking him.

Alice held her ground. "Denver, you don't really want me any more than I want you." She looked from one brother to the other. "This isn't even *about* me."

She gave them each another push before flinging her hands up. "Figure it out for yourselves. I'm leaving."

She stalked off, barging past a stable hand who was leading a horse inside.

Kyle opened and closed his fists. He glanced at his brother before swinging his head away in disgust. "Why did you do it?"

"Because you're not—" Denver cut himself off. There was something strange in his eyes.

"What?"

Denver gave his head a shake. He spat blood. "You're not better'n me."

"Have I ever said I was?"

"You act like it."

"You *think* I do."

Denver grabbed his hat off the cement and slapped it against his thigh. "Yeah."

A major concession.

"I'm sorry I hit you," Kyle said. "I shouldn't have."

"Hell, yeah, you should have." Denver put on his hat and puffed out his chest. The cocky grin was back. "I was making a play for your gal."

Kyle didn't speak. Down the aisle, the sound of the horse's hooves on the cement reminded him of his position.

Denver made a chuffing sound. "She was right, you know. I don't want her. She doesn't want me." He lifted the saddle off the floor. "So what're you waiting for? Go get her."

Kyle put out his hand.

Denver hesitated a couple of seconds before swinging the saddle down by his side with one hand wrapped beneath the cantle. He reached out with the other.

The brothers shook. Their eyes met.

"You're gonna have a helluva shiner," Denver said.

"What about that fat lip of yours?"

Denver's smile cracked the dried blood. "I'll get some tender loving care."

"Not from any of the guests."

"Nah. I got my eye on one of the maids. A sweet little *chica* with black eyes."

Kyle just shook his head. His glance landed on their interested observer, the stable hand who'd come in at the end of the fight. Could be trouble, Kyle supposed, but at the moment he couldn't make himself care all that much.

"Go on," Denver said. "I'll talk to him."

They shared another look.

"Thanks." Kyle said. "Thanks…brother."

ALICE HAD HOPED to slip inside the condo unobserved, but Harriet Humbert waylaid her at the door. "Hank's been asking about you. He wondered if you'd like a night out on the town."

Alice's head was not in the moment. She couldn't think of a single excuse. "Oh, I don't know…"

"Listen, toots. Hank may not be the dreamboat type like Mr. Jarreau, but the guy's a catch. He's got a house and a cabin cruiser, no STDs or ex-wives, and he's even trained in Krav Maga for the past six years. He can take down a man twice his size."

The thought that most were twice his size popped into Alice's head. The idea of Henry Humbert, accountant, karate-chopping at some man-mountain's knee made her smile. "I'm sure Hen—Hank's a great guy. Thank him for the invitation, but I'm planning to stay in tonight."

"That's no way to vacation."

"Yes, well, it seems I've been vacationing too hard. I need recovery time."

"Uh-huh." Harrie scrinched her elfin face into even more creases. "We've all heard about your late dates."

"Late? I was home by eight o'clock."

"Home, but not alone, heh?"

"What are you implying?"

"Never mind." Harrie poked out a sharp elbow. "So what about tomorrow night?" She saved Alice from concocting an excuse by correcting herself. "No, I just remembered—that's no good. Plans are brewing."

Alice didn't pick up on the hint; she was too thrilled to have an out. "Aw, and I'm leaving the next day. You'll have to tell Hank I'm sorry. Maybe next time."

She escaped, somewhat disappointed in herself for being less than straightforward about her lack of interest in Harrie's nephew.

Her mind was still replaying Kyle's confrontation with his brother.

Emotions had been raw, the testosterone flying. She wasn't accustomed to violence, but she had to admit the fight had been exciting.

Kyle had been forceful. Direct. Unrestrained. Passionate.

Whether or not that applied to her or only to his complicated family relationships was another question.

WHEN THE DOORBELL rang after ten that night, she looked through the peephole and saw a piece of coconut cake, fish-eyed to appear as large as a raft. She leaned her forehead against the door for a moment before saying, "Who is it?"

The foam take-out box opened and closed like a maw. "Dessert." Kyle's voice.

"I didn't order any dessert."

"Fred sent me. This other guy's just the courier."

"I don't eat cakes that speak." But she opened the door. It almost hurt to see Kyle, all suited up again. Her chest tightened.

Then she noticed his black eye. Automatically she reached to touch the puffed purple skin. He turned his face away.

"Does it hurt?"

"Some."

A hollow opened in her stomach, even though she'd snacked her way through the remains of her kitchen stock. "Your people were arriving today."

"Yes. I just finished dinner with them."

"They must have wondered about that eye."

"I made up a story about a horse kicking me." He smiled, crinkling his eyes and making him wince. "You're tuned in to the gossip. Have you heard otherwise?"

Of course he'd be worried about that. Why shouldn't he be?

She mumbled something negative, not wanting to explain that she'd been holed up all evening.

He worked the box again. "I have lemon filling and white buttercream frosting with toasted coconut."

She laughed. "Stop it."

"I'm here for you. Just for you."

She took the cake. "Which of you was speaking then?"

Kyle kissed her cheek. Briefly. "Me."

She wished he'd lingered. "Have you tried ice on that eye?"

"There was no time. After I left the stable, I had to

change my suit and drive to Phoenix to meet a plane." He made a face. "Lani wanted to put cover-up on me."

"Bad idea. You'd've looked like a man with a black eye wearing makeup." She left the door to go to the kitchen. "Come in. I'll treat you to half a piece of cake and an ice pack." She glanced over her shoulder. "That is, if you're willing to stay for a while. I guarantee that someone from the condo crew will have noticed."

He didn't hesitate. "I'll take the risk."

She returned with a tray of supplies, and they arranged themselves on the couch. "This time, I'm the doctor." She went up on her knees. Ministering was a good excuse to get her hands on him. "Lean back and loosen that tie. Put your feet up." She gave his chest a pat. "Better, hmm?"

"Mmm."

She slapped on the baggie of ice she'd prepared.

He flinched. "Damn, that's cold."

"That's right." She pressed his hand to the ice. "Hold it there while I eat my cake."

He watched her out of one eye. "I thought you'd be more sympathetic."

"Me, too." She stabbed the fork into the cake, coming away with a huge bite. "What was the big idea, fighting with Denver like that?"

"You were kissing him—" Kyle started to say. She stuffed a large forkful of cake into his mouth.

She waved the fork. "*He* was kissing *me*. That should have been obvious."

"It was," he said through his mouthful.

"Well, then. Why did you start swinging?"

"No excuses. I was jealous, no matter who was kissing whom. I just plain lost it."

She put down the plate. "Mr. Discipline lost it?"

"And I may not get it back."

"What's *it?*"

His chest expanded as he inhaled. He was leaning back against the corner of the couch, both arms raised, one hand propping his head up, the other keeping the bag of ice in place. Butterflies fluttered in her stomach. The smear of buttercream on his bottom lip made him seem especially vulnerable.

"My idea that I can control everything in my life, I suppose. Especially myself."

"No one can. Not all the time."

"I should have realized that last night." His eye was closed. He didn't move. "I lost it then, too."

She couldn't resist any longer. She crawled up beside him and snuggled against his side. He was trying so hard.

His arm curved around her. "Alice Potter," he said to the ceiling. "Who'd have thought you would be my undoing?"

She thought of the beautiful and seductive Jenna Malloy. *Does not compute.*

"There's more to you than any other woman I've known," he added.

She put her face against his chest and squeezed her eyes shut in happiness. "It's all these desserts."

"Don't." He dropped the bag of ice and put his cold hand to her cheek, raising her face to kiss her.

Once, coconut-flavored.

Twice, Kyle-flavored.

"I'm being serious," he said. "You're something special to me, Alice. I really do…like you. A lot." He tilted his head back. "And I hope that your leaving doesn't mean we won't ever see each other again."

She nestled against him, disappointed that he hadn't been able to take the full step into "I love you."

I'm not ready for that, either, she decided. *And besides, just saying the words without living them means nothing.* Like her former fiancé had.

"You can send postcards," she said, trying to sound light and carefree.

He hugged her. "I'll send plane tickets."

"Oh, well, *that'd* be worth a thanks."

He didn't miss the dry intonation. "What?"

She lifted her head. "Your postcard this morning." Had it only been this morning? "You wrote 'Thanks.'" She shrugged. "I wasn't sure what you meant by that."

Kyle frowned.

"Thanks for the roll in the hay?" she guessed. "No, I suppose that'd be more Denver's line."

"Don't bring him into this."

"No? Maybe it was thanks for the memories, then."

Kyle gave her a small shake. "You goof."

Was she? She didn't know. "You're a hard man to read."

"I'll spell it out for you." He straightened, keeping her with him as he traced the letter *T* across her chest. "Thanks for taking the trip to Elk River with me."

"That was—"

With his thumb, he pressed her lips closed. "*H.* Thanks for having the patience and compassion to deal with my family. They might not be the best people in the world, but they're always going to be part of my life."

"Even your—" He wagged a finger and she stopped, although one of these days she was going to ask about his father. She'd lost both her parents now, and she had a hard time accepting that the hole in Kyle's heart couldn't be filled.

He traced an *A* that dipped below the scoop-neck of her tank. "Thanks for being Alice."

His desire was so evident that she tried really hard to let herself believe. He didn't want Jenna. He wanted her, Alice.

She took his hand and placed it over her breast. He cupped it, rubbing his thumb back and forth over the hardened crest, then traced a tingling letter *N*.

"Thanks for not giving up on me, even when I was being…" The rest of his words were lost as his mouth moved to her neck. The straps of her top fell, giving his tongue access to her breast. His tongue's wandering path might have been the letter *K*.

"Thanks for all the kissing," he said hotly into her ear, and they both laughed low in their throats.

By then, they had lost all attempts at propriety and were horizontal on the sofa, she in her pajama pants and he in his tailored suit. He lifted off her top, tangling her arms above her head with it so she was half-naked beneath him.

He lowered his mouth. She arched into the heat and pleasure of his kiss.

Two-fingered, he drew a long sinuous *S* from her collarbone to her navel. "Thanks. Thanks for saving me from myself."

She reached between his legs. "I don't know about that, but I sure wouldn't mind saving you just for me."

After that, they had nothing more to say. He removed his jacket while she unbuckled his belt, unzipped his trousers. His eyes were on hers while he sheathed himself. She had a moment of startling clarity, acknowledging just how badly she wanted to keep him, before his tongue and his fingers were inside her, stoking her desire.

She shuddered. Cried out, gripping his shoulders, as he filled her.

They were together now. Right now. Was *forever* necessary?

CHAPTER FOURTEEN

THEY'D MADE no plans, and she'd known he'd be busy impressing the board of executives, so Alice hadn't expected to see Kyle that day. Her last day. Tomorrow she'd be leaving at 10:00 a.m. for the airport.

He might show up at her door late tonight, she supposed. In secret. When it was safe. And she'd let him in. There was no use denying that.

And yet…

Keep in touch. Why did that sound so lame?

Because it was.

Fresh from her second shower of the day, Alice wandered around the condo, straightening and polishing. She'd been told that maids would come in after she was gone, but she couldn't bear to leave a mess. Her mother had been fussy like that, to the point of asking Alice to tidy up her hospital room on the day she died.

Alice looked at her reflection in the sliding glass door. "Hey, Mom."

I'm traveling. I'm being adventurous. Maybe it's not everything I built it up to be—because I'm not really, truly, a sporty kind of girl—but it's been amazing all the same.

"I won't stay on Osprey Island for the rest of my life, like you did."

The doorbell rang and, reprieved, she hurriedly

yanked the sheer over the glass. She didn't have to decide what to do with the rest of her life right then.

She was expecting Harrie or Mags or Mary Grace, but it was Chloe, spiffy in her crisp white PM jacket and black skirt. After Alice had said so, Chloe made a face. "I've been starched for our visitors."

"How's the review going?" Alice asked, trying to sound nonchalant, since she wasn't supposed to be informed on the subject.

"I wouldn't know. I put on a big smile and trailed along for part of the activities tour, but my superior did the talking, along with Mr. Jarreau."

Chloe paused. Was it Alice's imagination, or was Chloe looking at her expectantly?

"They'll be in meetings all afternoon with the department heads. Then the big powwow is tomorrow. We won't know the verdict until after they leave." Chloe looked at Alice again. "Lani will spread the word."

Alice smiled. "Would you like a lemonade?"

"Is it hard lemonade? If ever there was a day I'd be driven to drink, this would be it."

"No, sorry. Only sugared."

"That'll do." Chloe talked over the clatter of Alice dropping ice cubes into glasses. "Excuse me for going on like that. I don't suppose you're interested in the ins and outs of hotel management."

"I don't mind." Alice brought in a tray and set it down in front of the sofa, self-conscious about the night before. She and Kyle, having sex right there. "I, um, hope the resort passes its inspection with flying colors."

Chloe drank, still eyeing Alice as if they shared a secret. "You're so discreet. I commend you."

Alice went still. "What do you mean?"

"The *triangle*. It's all over the resort, at least among the staff."

Triangle! "There's no triangle."

"Then it's not true that the Jarreau brothers fought over you at the stable?"

Alice winced. "Technically—"

Chloe crowed. *"Alice!"*

"Wait. No. Really. It's not like that."

"Oh, yeah? *Everybody* saw the black eye. And I heard that Denver's got a split lip and bruised knuckles."

Alice clenched her hands, trying to hold herself in, but after a minute she gave up. "Poor Kyle. Do you know if the board members heard any rumors? Are they asking questions? I'll die if I've ruined things for him."

"Gavin told Melina, who told the desk crew, but so far the board doesn't suspect a thing."

"Oh, God." Alice was appalled. "So everyone else knows?"

"It's the hot topic."

"But do people actually think…" She stopped, uncertain how to ask. If Harrie and her gang knew about Kyle's late-night visits, likely everyone did.

"Don't look so worried," Chloe said, taking pity on her. "Mr. Jarreau's respected because he's fair. Most of the staff even like him. No one's out to take him down." She chuckled. "But there are some who are thrilled to see him getting some of his own back. The fraternization policy, you know. It's stung a few employees."

Alice sank lower. "I've got to go. That's the thing to do—just leave the resort now." She inched forward to the edge of the cushions. "I'll call the front desk, see if they can get me an earlier flight—"

"You can't." Chloe put out a restraining hand. "I

didn't even get to my reason for stopping by. You're invited to a goodbye dinner tonight at Oasis de la Luna. Rivka and Fred are planning the dessert."

"For me?"

"We want your last night here to be special."

Special. What if she accepted the invitation and then Kyle called?

But he wouldn't, she decided. Not with everyone gossiping and his promotion on the line.

If she couldn't disappear, the next best choice was to get busy. She'd even go on the moonlight trail ride, if she had to.

People would look at her, ordinary Alice Potter of Osprey Island, and they'd look at Kyle, who had everything going for him, and they'd *have* to doubt the rumors.

"That sounds nice," she said, "as long as it's a small, quiet dinner. I wouldn't want to attract a lot of attention."

Chloe's smile didn't waver. "You'll have a great time." Perhaps she read Alice's discomfort, because she quickly changed the subject, asking about the morning activity she'd booked—a hike up Camelback Mountain with a small group from the Oasis.

"I climbed right into a cold shower when I got back, but it was worth every drop of sweat," Alice said. She described the hike to Chloe as she walked the woman to the door.

After she'd gone, Alice became reflective again.

The trip to Arizona was both a beginning and an end. She'd fulfilled her mother's final bequest at the same time as she'd opened a new world for herself. She understood that what she wanted didn't necessarily have to include rock climbing or skydiving. She simply wasn't a daredevil.

What she truly craved was a full life. To be open to adventure, experience, emotion, in whatever form they came.

And to share it with a partner.

If that wasn't Kyle, if all they shared from now on were postcards, she'd have to accept that and find a way to move on. She wouldn't let herself crawl into a hole the way she had after Stewart.

Which would take courage, a quality she now knew she had.

"WE'RE IN TROUBLE," Lani said, coming into Kyle's office as soon as the board members had been escorted to their suites for afternoon downtime.

"I thought it went well," he replied. "They're not just looking at my black eye the way they were last night."

"It's not them we have to worry about. At least not yet." Lani collapsed into the chair in front of his desk with a grateful sigh. She'd been run off her feet all day. As soon as the review was over, he was rewarding her with a week off.

"Is my intervention absolutely crucial?" he asked. The lengthy tour of the resort and the meet-and-greet with the various department heads had been window dressing. The meat of the review was in the reports they'd present tomorrow morning, followed by the number-crunching evaluation of profit and loss.

Kyle wasn't worried. His profit margin was healthy, up seven percent from the previous fiscal year.

Only a disaster could derail him now.

Lani reached down to ease off her open-toed pumps. "Ahhh. That's better."

He'd warned her not to wear heels. But she'd wanted to show off her pedicure, and considering the way

Carson Walmsley had been distracted all morning by the sight of Lani's toes, Kyle wasn't bucking the choice. He'd even begun to wonder if the man had a foot fetish.

Kyle rubbed his forehead.

"The staff is talking."

"And that's never good." He scowled at the chief perpetrator. "Do I have to ask what they're talking about?"

She gave him a despairing look. "Fighting with your brother the day before the board arrived? What *were* you thinking?"

"Clearly, I wasn't." Despite what he'd said to Alice, he'd been claiming the shiner was a basketball injury— an elbow to the eye. He'd even got Gavin to back him up. "Who told you?"

"I heard it from everyone."

"Damn my brother," Kyle said, though he knew he couldn't hold Denver completely accountable. The stable hand might have sworn he wouldn't talk, but one leak was all it took.

He yanked off his tie. "What's the damage?"

Lani managed to seem both curious and sympathetic. "There are about a dozen versions. The details get wilder by the minute. But the gist of it is that you and Denver were fighting over a woman. Some people are claiming it was Jenna Malloy. But most of them say Alice Potter."

Lani's eyes twinkled. "My guess is the latter."

He shrugged. "Either way, they're both guests."

"But at least Jenna is a former girlfriend. You didn't originally meet her here at the resort. I'm betting Walmsley wouldn't care if it was her. He'd congratulate you on your good taste." Lani stuck her tongue out. "He's a slimeball, if you ask me."

"He liked your toes."

"Ew, I know. He asked me where I got my pedicure, so I gave the spa a rousing recommendation. He'll probably book an appointment and drool all over the customers. The spa girls will come after me with cuticle scissors."

Kyle couldn't summon up much of a sense of humor. "Don't do anything rash. I may need your toes tomorrow."

"I'd do anything for you, boss, but I wouldn't do that." A deep sigh. "Seriously," she said, "if one word of the rumors reaches the board…"

"The thing is—it's not a rumor."

"It's the truth?" Lani squealed. "I thought it might be, but when I heard that you were supposedly seen sneaking into Alice's condo at all hours, I thought for sure the gossip must be off course."

Lani stopped when she saw his face. She blinked several times. "*That's* true, too?"

Kyle motioned for silence. "I don't want to hear any more. Just tell me how I can keep the gossip away from the board."

Lani's eyebrows shot up. "Build one helluva gigantic dam."

"In one day? That'd take dynamite." He brooded.

Lani studied him, keeping quiet for a long beat. "You're serious about her."

"How can you tell?" He thought he'd been pretty damn cool about everything. Until yesterday.

"Easy question." His secretary ticked off the points with a clarity he used to appreciate. "You didn't care about the cake or the wedding crashing. You went ATV riding with her and you came back with dust in every nook and cranny and didn't care. You tolerated your brother's needling. You didn't spare a glance for Jenna."

"That's no proof."

"Wait. Here's the biggie. You took Alice to meet your family." Lani pointed at him. "And then you *stopped* tolerating your brother." She paused. "I'd even say you're not as gung ho over the performance review as I expected."

"Hey, now, *that's* not true."

"No? Remember last year? You called me to the office at 3:00 a.m. because you found a misplaced comma in the purchasing report."

"You're exaggerating."

Lani pinched two fingers together. "Only a tiny bit." Her smile was growing much too wide. "*Something's* changed your attitude, that's all I'm saying."

He stared her down.

"It's not only getting laid," she added.

He narrowed his eyes. "I've been laid before."

"That's right." She stared right back at him. "And it's different this time."

Damn. She was right.

"Ask Gavin. He'll tell you."

"Gavin's as gone on romance as you are."

"Romance, hmm?"

He put his head in his hands. "Forget I said that."

She stood and picked up her shoes with a small groan. "Sure I will. But can you?"

"For the next twenty-four hours? Hell, yeah."

Long after Lani had gone, he was still trying to persuade himself that was true. All he'd have to do was play it cool and stay away from Alice Potter.

"I'm meeting Chloe Weston," Alice told the maître d' at the entrance to Oasis de la Luna. "Alice Potter."

"Ah, yes." After fourteen days, he finally seemed to

recognize her. He even smiled. "This way, please, Miss Potter."

They walked through the main room. Alice's eyes darted from table to table, but she couldn't see Kyle.

The maître d' opened a door to a private room. "Your party, Miss Potter."

A cheer went up. "Surprise!"

She stood, staring.

The room was filled with everyone she'd met at the resort. Rivka and Fred and the catering manager, several well-tanned couples she'd chatted with at the pool, numerous acquaintances from the condos. There was Denver and Lani and Ramon the bartender and the desert guide, plus a bunch of other staffers she'd met along the way. Even the editor and photographer from the bridal magazine and several of their models.

Everyone!

Except Kyle.

Chloe bounded toward her, tossing a streamer in the air. There were also balloons, champagne and a banner that read *We'll Miss You, Alice.*

"It's your farewell party," Chloe exclaimed. She was hopping with energy. "Are you surprised?"

"I'm completely stunned." Alice dragged a couple of streamers out of her hair. "I don't know what to say. There are so many of you."

"Of course. You've made a lot of friends."

Harrie and Mags pushed to the front of the crowd. In his stentorian voice, Walter St. Gregory was trying to organize a sing-along of "For She's a Jolly Good Fellow," but most of the guests were too busy swarming Alice to notice.

Mags gave Alice a voluminous hug. "You didn't

think we'd let you get away without a party, did you? We are the Cocktail Shakers, after all."

Harrie handed her a glass of champagne, confiding, "Hank's here. He can't wait to see you."

Alice was flying high enough that she nodded happily and looked for him, but the unassuming little man seemed lost in the crowd.

Unlike Denver. He'd worn his cowboy hat and the silver buckle with a new pair of jeans. His shirt bore piping and fancy embroidery.

He doffed the hat. "The old place won't be the same without you, Miss Allie."

She giggled. One swallow, and the champagne was already getting to her. "I suspect you'll get along fine, Denver."

"Yeah, but Loco's missin' you already."

She touched his cheek. "How're you doing?" The cut on his lip was red and swollen.

He gave her a one-sided grin. "Not fired yet."

"You and Kyle need to make up to each other."

"Don't worry." He lowered his voice. "Unless he catches you'n'me kissin' again, we're gonna get along just dandy."

She gave him a playful push. "Then you'd better stay away."

Denver lifted his head. "Where *is* Kyle?"

"I'm sure he's busy."

There was an apology in the way Denver looked at her. "For a smart man, my brother's awful dumb."

Alice could only shake her head. She was trying not to think of Denver's warning about how Kyle would cut her out of his life. She definitely didn't want to admit her fear that it was happening right then and there.

She downed her champagne in between greetings and hugs. The crowd propelled her toward the tables set up along the wall. Rivka and Fred, in their chef coats, presented her with a cake in the shape of a saguaro cactus. The chorus of "Jolly Good Fellow" finally got off the ground. Afterward, everyone called for a speech.

Their warmth and hospitality had overwhelmed Alice. "I'm at a loss for words," she admitted. "Years ago, I used to stand in front of a class of ten-year-olds and I never—"

"This ain't much different," called Denver.

Alice laughed along with the crowd. "In those days, I had lesson plans. I'm not so good off the cuff." She took a big breath. "All I can say is thanks to every one of you for being part of my vacation. It's changed my life." Her eyes welled. "I'll never forget my time at the Oasis."

There were more cheers, a round of toasts, jokes and laughter. The guests swarmed the lavish buffet, but Alice didn't have much of an appetite. She helped herself to a plate of food and nibbled at it, but mostly she talked, snapped photos and took down addresses and cell phone numbers. She was invited to visit Oconomowoc, Wisconsin, and Oxford, Mississippi, on her next adventure. Ramon brought in several pitchers of what he called Alice-in-Oasisland prickly-pear rum punch. The talk and laughter grew even louder.

After a few hours, the party began to break up. Some employees had to report for work, a number of the guests wanted to go on to the nightclub, while others decided to join the moonlight trail ride.

Alice was supposed to go on the ride, too, but she was

reluctant. She'd hugged Chloe goodbye and was slowly making her way to the door when Kyle's secretary tapped her shoulder. "May I have a word?"

Alice's heart leaped into her throat. "Of course."

Lani drew her aside. "I wanted to speak to you all evening, but not with so many people around."

"What can I do for you?"

Lani's head bobbed. "Kyle doesn't know about this."

"The party?"

"Oh, no, he's aware of the party." At Alice's crest-fallen look, the secretary gave her a quick squeeze. "He wanted to come, but he simply couldn't."

Alice's murmur of understanding got stuck in her throat.

"You see, coming here would have put him in a compromising position he just can't risk right now."

"Or ever," Alice said stiffly.

"You know about the rumors?" the secretary asked.

"Chloe told me. Tell Kyle I'm sorry. I didn't want to cause him trouble."

"You'll see him yourself."

"No, it's best if I don't see him, don't you think?" Although the farewell party hadn't been the quiet dinner she'd hoped for, it had turned out okay. No one had mentioned Kyle. Not even Harrie.

"I couldn't say what's best." But Lani looked as if she was biting her tongue.

"What did you want to talk to me about?"

"Like I said, Kyle doesn't know I'm speaking to you. He wouldn't want me to, but—" Lani shrugged "—I'm a busybody. I had to make sure you knew what was happening, that he wasn't neglecting you on purpose."

"But it *is* on purpose."

"Well, then, it's for the right purpose. But as soon as the review is over, things'll be different."

"I'll be gone by then. I'm leaving in the morning on the ten o'clock shuttle."

Lani was nonplussed. "Does Kyle know that?"

"I think so. He definitely knows I'm leaving to-morrow." Alice made a helpless gesture. "So you see, between the rumors and the board and my departure, there's no time left. But that's all right, really. I don't expect…expect him to—"

She clamped her lips together. "It's all right," she blurted again, when it was glaringly obvious that it was not.

"Oh, honey." Lani's dark eyes filled with sympathy. "I've only made it worse. When will I learn to keep my big mouth shut?" She patted Alice's arm. "Don't give up. Kyle might come through for you. He really is a good man. It's just that he's a stickler about reaching his goals. He's had to be, coming from where he did."

Alice stopped the secretary's dithering. "I know all about that. I really do understand."

Lani cocked her head, bright-eyed again. "You know? About the mess with his sister, and how he got his mother to retire? About him buying the house for them in Elk River?"

Alice nodded.

"Well, my goodness. If he trusts you that much, he *must* be—"

"There you are! Kyle's Alice, isn't that right?" The editor from the bridal magazine looked her over with more approval than she'd previously shown. "I have a little memento for you."

Alice was still stuck on the phrase *Kyle's Alice*.
"I, uh—"

"There's no need to deny it." The woman's laughter
boomed, making several employees, who were clearing
the buffet, look up. She waved the large manila envelope
in her hand. "I've got the proof right here."

She presented Alice with the envelope, then tossed
her long knotted scarf over one shoulder and sailed out
of the room while Alice was still stammering her thanks.

Alice tore it open and took out a photograph. *The*
photograph. She and Kyle, kissing on the bridge. There
were no brides in the picture, just them.

"It's lovely," Lani said.

"We were supposed to be background." Studying the
photo, seeing the love between them, Alice was glad that
for once she hadn't been background. Not the substitute.

The real thing.

Whether or not Kyle knew it, she did.

She held the photograph against her chest. "Thanks,
Lani. I'm going to be okay. Even if I don't see him
again, Kyle knows how I feel." She glanced at the photo
again. "I promise you, I'm not leaving sad."

Alice walked out. *Courage,* she told herself as she
entered the dining room, still the onesome but not quite
so lonesome. *I've got it.*

She stopped beside an empty table to pick up the
streamer that was trailing off her shoe. A woman's sultry
laugh drew her attention across the room.

Jenna Malloy. She hadn't come to the party and now
Alice knew why. The model was seated at a table with
several obviously important people.

And Kyle.

Jenna reached across the table to touch his hand, but

her eyes were on Alice. "Look, Kyle, we've missed the party."

He yanked his hand away.

"Is it over already?" Jenna asked Alice. "We intended to stop by."

"Yes, it's over." A peculiar sense of numbness had overcome Alice. She couldn't feel her body, only the rasp of air in her throat as she tried to breathe. She dropped the streamer.

She looked down. The photograph.

Why hadn't she seen it before? The pose was similar to the one printed in the newspaper back home, the portrait of Alice's supposed fiancé announcing his engagement to another woman. She'd been numb then, too. Numb and dumb.

"What party?" said one of the men at the table, his deep voice instantly commanding attention. He was an older version of Kyle—well groomed, tailored, authoritative.

Kyle stood. "It's nothing, Mr. Walmsley. A going-away party for one of the guests."

Nothing? Alice winced.

"I see." The man's gaze went past Alice to Lani, arriving beside her. "Mrs. Steen. How nice to see you again. You must join us."

Kyle walked toward Alice. His eyes were dark, beseeching. "What's that?" he asked, looking at her hand.

"It's nothing." She knew he wasn't rekindling a romance with Jenna, but for the moment, that didn't matter. All she could think about was how much this felt like she was being jilted all over again. Only this time, she was losing out not to another woman, but to a promotion.

Without looking, certainly without feeling, she tore the photo in half. The pieces fell to the floor.

She fled.

CHAPTER FIFTEEN

From professional business conferences to intimate wedding receptions, the Prince Montez Oasis Resort offers its guests something special for every occasion.

August 4
Dear Alice,
It's one minute after midnight, so it's official. You're leaving Arizona today. Since you'll beat this postcard home, I don't know why you're bothering to write it, except that it seems like a good way to end the vacation. At least, a much better way than what happened a couple of hours ago. Welcome home.
A.
P.S.: Sorry I couldn't think of anything encouraging to write to you except, maybe, that this too shall pass? Or as a wise person once said, it's all water under the bridge.

ALICE GROANED. *Water under the bridge?* How appropriate, given the photo she'd torn in half. That seemed like an action worthy of a drama queen now. She was already sorry she'd done it in front of members of Kyle's board. But at the time there'd been nothing unreasonable about the action. All she'd felt was loss.

She wrote her address on the postcard—Pine Cone Cottage, 18 Shore Road, Osprey Island, Maine—and stuck on a stamp.

There. Finished.

Her clothes were packed. She was ready to go.

She only had to get through the next ten hours without coming apart. After she was safe at home, she could begin to untwist the knots in her heart, and maybe she'd find that she wasn't wrong. The vacation *had* changed her.

In a good way.

The doorbell rang. She dropped the postcard. *Don't answer it.*

Then the loud knocking began. She flinched. He must be using his fist, not caring who heard.

"Alice?" Kyle called. "Please open the door."

She walked toward it. *Stay strong.*

"Alice, please. I know it's late. I wanted to come right away, but..."

Aha. Standing beside the door, she covered her face. *There's the rub. With Kyle, there'd always be a but.* His need for more success would always come first.

"I can explain. Let me in."

No. She put her hand against the wood. *Not this time.*

"Are you there?" She heard a soft thud on the other side of the door, which moved beneath her hand. "At least let me know you can hear me."

She turned her back, leaned against the door. She didn't make a sound, but she couldn't walk away, either.

"Alice, I know you're there. I went to the stable. Denver said you didn't show up for the trail ride. All I'm asking is that you listen, okay? Will you listen?"

She'd listened to Stewart. His excuses for hurting her. *He'd* felt better afterward.

"I went into the restaurant to drop by your party. But Walmsley saw me and asked me to join them for a drink. I couldn't say no. Then Jenna came along." He exhaled. "We weren't together."

Alice had figured that out, more or less. Even if he'd *wanted* to have her join them, it wouldn't have been appropriate. She was the guest. The holiday romance. On her way to checking out. Why should he risk going public with her?

There was a long silence. "Alice?" Kyle said, practically in her ear. She shivered. He'd put his mouth to the door. "Are you there?"

She crossed her arms. *I'm here. But not for much longer.*

"Please," he said. "Let me in. I'll make it up to you."

Oh, no. Not that way.

"Alice?"

Don't open it, don't open it. Not this time.

"Alice." He pushed. The door pulsed against her. "I can't see you tomorrow. This is our last chance."

Last chance. Last risk. Did she dare take it?

"All right. I don't blame you." His voice was low and grating. He sounded beaten. "I'll say goodbye. I hope you're listening." His hands moved across the door. "I know you're listening. I can feel you."

"I can feel you," she whispered too softly for him to hear.

"This is goodbye, but it's not forever. Please don't let it be forever."

It's not my risk to take. It's his.

"After tomorrow, I'll know where I stand." There was a catch in his voice, but he cleared his throat and went on. "If I get the promotion, I'll be moving to the company's headquarters in New York. That's closer to you, if you stay in Maine. We could see each other."

He was making an attempt, but he'd be a big wheel, expected to uphold a certain image. She couldn't imagine fitting into that world. Jenna Malloy, though, she'd make the perfect executive wife. Polished and confident where Alice was shy and uncertain.

"Don't you think?" he asked, sounding uncertain himself.

Honestly? I don't know what to think. Maybe she was being too hard on him. She hadn't exactly worn her heart on her sleeve, either, after the disaster that had been Stewart.

But she had been ready to move forward. Unlike Kyle.

She tilted her head back, closed her eyes. Still, why not open the door? Talk to him?

She heard him take a breath. "Or if I don't get the promotion…"

Her eyes flashed open. *It'll be my fault. Or partly mine. I can't live with that.*

The truth hit her hard, even though at the back of her mind she'd known all along. They could talk all night, but he wasn't going to commit. He was still too careful, too guarded.

This really was goodbye.

Alice dropped her face into her hands, stifling a sob. On the other side of the door, Kyle went on for a while longer, but she'd stopped listening.

He wasn't going to say what she needed to hear.

KYLE STARED DOWN the boardroom table. Proctor, Garson, Obermeyer and, at the foot, Walmsley. He knew their first names, their middle names, their spouses' names, their children's and pets' names. He knew their hobbies, their sports teams, their political affiliations. Hell, he knew what snacks they wanted stocked in their minibars and what drinks they ordered at the bar. He did not know what color and style of underwear they preferred, but he could have made a good guess.

Did he know Alice as well?

The underwear, yes. He almost smiled. Comfortable cotton, but not old-lady-style. Matching bras. Bikinis in pink and lavender.

But her family? Her mother's name was Dorothy, but he'd forgotten the names of the brother and the niece and nephews. She had a cat, he recalled, a cat that used to be her mother's.

He squinted. He *did* know her. The details were coming back to him.

She'd have a glass of wine or champagne now and then, but two made her tipsy. The night he met her, she'd ordered prickly-pear rum punch at the bar. She liked healthy snacks such as granola bars and trail mix, but she ordered a fancy dessert every time she ate out. Her favorite movie was something with Johnny Depp. But what was the title again?

Benny and Joon, that was it.

The cat was called Snowball.

Her middle name was Georgina, after a great-grandfather who'd died in a war.

She was a Scrabble and Parcheesi whiz and she'd once run a 5K marathon for charity to prove to her students she could do it. She'd been voted Teacher of the Year the year before she had to quit. Her oldest friend had married a marine and moved to a military base overseas. Alice regretted that they'd lost touch. Her best friend ran a bakery on Osprey Island called Suzy Q's.

Each detail Kyle remembered came with a growing sense of awareness. By the time he'd finished, he was a goner. He started to rise, realized where he was, and sat down. But he had to do *something*.

Iris Proctor cleared her throat. The silence after his opening speech had grown too long.

Walmsley was giving Kyle the stink eye. He wished he could give it back, the way he'd stood up for his family as a schoolboy, before he'd become so law-abiding.

Instead, he nodded at Gavin. "Gavin Brill, my assistant manager, will present the first report."

There was a smattering of applause as Gavin rose from the executive staff lined up on the opposite side of the table. He shot a look at Kyle before turning to the flat-screen monitor where their charts and graphs would appear. "If you'll turn to page seven in your report…"

Kyle didn't open his booklet. He knew it by heart.

His gut gave a kick. Did he know Alice by heart?

He put his hands on the table, then folded them near his chin so the cuff of his shirt would inch away from the face of his watch. Nine-forty-eight. The meeting had started late, what with Walmsley hovering near Lani at the coffeepot.

Nine-forty-nine. Alice had said she was leaving in the morning. For all he knew, she might already be gone.

Nine-fifty. He didn't know the exact time of her flight, but this meeting would last for hours. Lani had arranged a catered lunch. There was no possibility of making it to the airport in time to see Alice off.

He'd known that. It wasn't as though he hadn't tried

to make amends. He'd talked until his throat was raw, standing outside her door like a dog begging for a bone.

What more did she want from him?

Gavin droned on. "On page twelve, you'll see the overview of amenity expenditures..."

Walmsley looked bored. His gaze drifted toward Kyle, who hurriedly flipped open the report to make himself seem invested in the proceedings. The first page was heavy with a paper-clipped photograph and a Post-it from Lani.

The photo had been torn in two pieces and then taped back together. With a jolt he remembered Alice in the restaurant, ripping something in half. He'd been focused on her disappointed face. He hadn't thought to look at what she'd torn.

Lani had.

Kyle stared at the photo, only vaguely mindful that Iris Proctor, on his immediate right, was doing the same. It was Alice and him, on the bridge. Kissing. Just barely. Their lips had touched, but she hadn't yet closed her eyes. She was looking up at him with love and longing. The unadulterated hope in her expression stole every molecule of oxygen from his lungs.

The sounds of the boardroom became muffled. He could only hear the thud of his pulse, the ragged noise of his gasp for air, the *ping* of the flying paper clip as he yanked Lani's note free.

She'd written: "Alice is on the 10:00 a.m. airport shuttle."

His watch read nine-fifty-six. Kyle slammed his hands down on the table and thrust up from his chair. He seemed to be speaking into a wind tunnel. "I have to go."

Walmsley's head snapped back. His mouth opened and closed, and he said something that Kyle couldn't hear.

Kyle gestured to Gavin. Air rushed past his ears. Was he speaking?

Gavin grabbed him by the shoulders, following Kyle out the door. "You. Can't. Go."

"Take over for me. Say it was an emergency."

Suddenly Lani was there. "Where are my car keys?" he yelled, before realizing how loud his voice was. He shook his head, ready to apologize, but she was gone.

"Walmsley's a pit bull." Gavin's voice was also raised. "He'll demand to know—"

"So tell him. I don't care."

"Tell him what?"

Lani was back. She tossed him the keys. Kyle raced through the hallway to the emergency stairs, shouting over his shoulder as he ran. "Tell him I'm breaking all the rules. Tell him to take the promotion and shove it. Tell him I'm going after Alice."

A BAKER'S DOZEN, Alice thought as she looked around the shuttle bus. Twelve senior citizens and me. *Isn't this where I came in?*

That wasn't strictly true. A middle-aged married couple—the Callahans—were also on the bus. She'd met them by the pool. They'd won a seven-day stay at the resort in a sweepstakes contest, then discovered in the fine print that the prize was only good for the off-season. They were still disgruntled but now also sunburned, saying loudly that they couldn't wait to get back home.

Alice wasn't leaving in the greatest of moods herself.

Mags, Mary Grace and Harrie were seated nearby, trying to engage her in conversation. They'd insisted on coming along to see her off. Said they enjoyed airport goodbyes, second only to wedding receptions.

She smiled fondly at them.

"Look," Mags announced, flinging out an arm ringed with bracelets that clacked like castanets. "She smiled!"

"Ah." Harrie squinted over the top of her sunglasses. "Now I recognize you as our Alice."

"I'm sorry for being a grump. It's hard to say goodbye."

Mary Grace reached a soothing hand across the seat. "Especially when you're leaving your heart behind."

Alice blushed. "My heart is right where it belongs. I've learned not to give it away that easily."

And how, she wondered, did that make her any different from Kyle?

Hadn't she stood on the other side of the door from him, refusing to open it? Wasn't she just as much a coward, even after all her justifications?

Sure, she was willing. But not willing enough to take the chance of going first.

Because what if she said "I love you," and he said "Thanks"?

Her eyes stung. They were probably bloodshot. She dug through her carry-on bag for her sunglasses.

"You can be sad if you want," Mary Grace said.

"Phooey." Harrie leaned into the aisle. "Lemme tell you, toots, *Hank* would treat you like a queen. Are you sure you don't want—"

A honking car interrupted the offer, the noise coming directly from behind the bus. One of the passengers said, "He's going to run right up our tailpipe."

"No, he's passing."

Heads craned, following the car as it swerved into the adjoining lane, still honking up a frenzy.

Alice glanced out the window from her slumped position. Sleek car, crazy driver.

She bolted upright. Dark blue Caddy, crazy male driver. "Kyle," she said. "Kyle."

Harrie climbed over Alice to see. "What the—"

"That's Kyle Jarreau," Mags announced. She waved her arms. "Yoo-hoo! Hello-o-o there!"

"Holy cats. He wants us to pull over." Harrie stood and made her way up the aisle to the driver, grabbing onto seats as she went.

Mary Grace slipped into the seat beside Alice. "Oh, Alice. It's so romantic. He's come for you."

She couldn't take her eyes off Kyle's car, which had pulled even with the front of the bus. She could see him motioning for the driver to pull over. "It's probably... probably just a..."

But she couldn't think of a single reason, other than her, that Kyle might have to stop the bus. No, her heart must be galloping faster than her thoughts, she told herself. There had to be some other explanation. He was supposed to be in a meeting.

The driver had slowed the bus and was pulling over to the side of the road. Harrie hung over the safety rail by the door. "He's coming!" she shouted to the back of the bus.

The passengers stirred, catching the air of excitement. Mags and Mary Grace sat forward, watching expectantly.

Alice didn't. Her eyes were closed. Her fingers, tucked into her armpits, crossed. She'd never wanted anything more than for Kyle to say, in front of the entire bus and the rest of the world, too, that he wanted her, needed her, couldn't be happy without her. That she wasn't just a holiday romance.

She heard the *whoosh* of the door opening. The sound of footsteps. The murmur of the passengers.

And then Kyle's voice. "Alice Potter."

A man at the back of the bus grumbled about the delay and was quickly hushed. Mary Grace burbled with excitement, nudging Alice's side.

Alice removed her sunglasses but was too wobbly in the knees to stand. Kyle was waiting in the aisle, so tall his head seemed to touch the ceiling.

Her throat seemed to be lined with sandpaper. "Kyle, what are you doing here? What about your meeting?"

"The meeting's not as important as I thought it was."

"Your promotion."

"I've done enough. Either I get it or I don't."

"But coming here? They'll find out about you and me, and how will you ever explain that away?"

"I don't want to explain it away." Kyle reached past Mary Grace. He took Alice's hand and she felt herself rising, almost floating, pulled toward him like a balloon on a string. "But I will explain it."

Mags clapped her hands. "Oh, do!"

Explain it to me, Alice said silently.

"I'll tell them I broke company policy," Kyle began. "I'll tell them the story of how one evening, I walked into the lobby and saw a woman who looked lost. But when I met her, I learned that she knew exactly where she was going and that, surprisingly enough, it was a journey I wanted to take right alongside her."

One of Kyle's hands was on her waist. She leaned into it. She gripped his arm. She needed him to hold on to. She always would.

"I will tell them that this woman made me see how stuffy I'd been. That displaying emotion wouldn't weaken me. She showed me how much more meaning my life would have with her in it. And I'll explain that I would rather risk losing my job than losing her, because no matter how fast it's happened or how crazy it seems—"

"I love you," Alice said. She just couldn't contain it any longer.

A chorus of sighs rose from the passengers.

"I'm sorry I didn't open the door," she went on. "That was dumb. I was afraid if I let you in I'd cave the way I used to do with Stewart when he'd make up his excuses for letting me down."

Kyle cringed. "I won't ever let you down again."

"It's not you." She couldn't quite catch her breath. "I never said—it was too humiliating—but Stewart, he left me in a very public way. Announcing his new engagement before he'd even told me. Until lately, I never really admitted to myself how much that affected the choices I'd made ever since. How safe I've played it."

"If I ever meet him, I'll pound him into the ground."

She laughed weakly. "No, no more fights. He's not important to me now."

"Good, because I'm going to make you forget he ever existed."

"How will you do that?"

"By telling you every day how much I love you." Kyle kissed her once, lightly on the lips. The emotion in his dark eyes said how much more he wanted, when they no longer had an audience. "And that I'm never letting you drive out of my life again."

Alice was finally able to breathe. "You're taking quite a gamble, making that promise. We've only known each other two weeks."

"Didn't you hear?" He led her by the hand to the front of the bus, toward the steps. "I'm the son of a gambling man. I recognize a jackpot when I win one."

He stepped down. She followed, swooping toward him with her hands on his shoulders, launching herself into the unknown even though she had no idea where she was going or what she'd do when she got there. But she did know how long the trip would be.

Forever.

Kyle lifted her up in his arms, carrying her off the bus with a flourish. The passengers applauded and cheered, led by Harrie and Mags and Mary Grace, who'd crowded into the doorway and were waving gaily as Kyle carried Alice away.

She was overwhelmed, her mind spinning at the thought of all that he'd put on the line just for her. She put her mouth near his ear and said the one simple word that was far more eloquent than she'd known.

"Thanks."

* * * * *

ALEXANDROS KAREDES, snow dusting the shoulders of his leather jacket and glittering like jewels in his dark hair, stood at the door. Maria felt the blood drain from her head.

"Good evening, Ms. Santos."

His voice was as she remembered it. Deep. Husky. Perfect English, but with the faintest hint of a Greek accent. And cold, as cold as it had been that awful morning she would never forget, when he'd accused her of horrible things, called her terrible names....

"Aren't you going to ask me in?"

She fought for composure. Last time they'd faced each other, they'd been on his turf. Now they were on hers. She was in command here, and that meant everything.

"There's a sign on the door downstairs," she said, her tone every bit as frigid as his. "It says, 'No soliciting or vagrants.'"

His lips drew back in a wolfish grin. "Very amusing."

"What do you want, Prince Alexandros?"

A tight smile eased across his mouth and it killed her that even now, knowing he was a vicious, arrogant man, she couldn't help but notice what a handsome mouth it was. Chiseled. Generous. Beautiful, like the rest of him, which made him living proof that beauty could, indeed, be only skin deep.

"Such formality, Maria. You were hardly so proper the last time we were together."

She knew his choice of words was deliberate. She felt her face heat; she couldn't help that but she damned well didn't have to let him lure her into a verbal sparring match.

"I'll ask you once more, your highness. What do you want?"

"Ask me in and I'll tell you."

"I have no intention of asking you in. Tell me why you're here or don't. It's your choice, just as it will be my choice to shut the door in your face."

He laughed. It infuriated her but she could hardly blame him. He was tall—six two, six three—and though he stood with one shoulder leaning against the door frame, hands tucked casually into the pockets of the jacket, his pose was deceptive. He was strong, with the leanly muscled body of a well-trained athlete.

She remembered his body with painful clarity. The feel of him under her hands. The power of him moving over her. The taste of him on her tongue.

Suddenly, he straightened, his laughter gone. "I have not come this distance to stand in your doorway," he said coldly, "and I am not going to leave until I am ready to do so. I suggest you stand aside and stop behaving like a petulant child."

A petulant child? Was that what he thought? This man who had spent hours making love to her and had then accused her of—of trading her body for profit?

Except it had not been love, it had been sex. And the sooner she got rid of him, the better.

She let go of the doorknob and stepped aside. "You have five minutes."

He strolled past her, bringing cold air and the scent

of the night with him. She swung toward him, arms folded. He reached past her, pushed the door closed, then folded his arms, too. She wanted to open the door again but she'd be damned if she was going to get into a who's-in-charge-here argument with him. She was in charge, and he would surely see a tussle over the ground rules as a sign of weakness.

Instead, she looked past him at the big clock above her work table.

"Ten seconds gone," she said briskly. "You're wasting time, your highness."

"What I have to say will take longer than five minutes."

"Then you'll just have to learn to economize. More than five minutes, I'll call the police."

Instantly, his hand was wrapped around her wrist. He tugged her toward him, his dark-chocolate eyes almost black with anger.

"You do that and I'll tell every tabloid shark I can contact about how Maria Santos tried to buy a five-hundred-thousand-dollar commission by seducing a prince." He smiled thinly. "They'll lap it up."

* * * * *

What will it take for this billionaire prince to realize he's falling in love with his mistress…?
Look for
BILLIONAIRE PRINCE, PREGNANT MISTRESS
by Sandra Marton
Available July 2009 from Harlequin Presents®.

We'll be spotlighting a different series every month throughout 2009 to celebrate our 60th anniversary.

Look for Harlequin® Presents in July!

TWO CROWNS, TWO ISLANDS, ONE LEGACY

A royal family, torn apart by pride and its lust for power, reunited by purity and passion

Step into the world of Karedes beginning this July with

BILLIONAIRE PRINCE, PREGNANT MISTRESS
by
Sandra Marton

Eight volumes to collect and treasure!

You're invited to join our Tell Harlequin Reader Panel!

By joining our new reader panel you will:

- Receive Harlequin® books—they are FREE and yours to keep with no obligation to purchase anything!
- Participate in fun online surveys
- Exchange opinions and ideas with women just like you
- Have a say in our new book ideas and help us publish the best in women's fiction

In addition, you will have a chance to win great prizes and receive special gifts! See Web site for details. Some conditions apply. Space is limited.

To join, visit us at

www.TellHarlequin.com.

REQUEST YOUR FREE BOOKS!

2 FREE NOVELS PLUS 2 FREE GIFTS!

HARLEQUIN®

Super Romance®

Exciting, emotional, unexpected!

YES! Please send me 2 FREE Harlequin® Superromance® novels and my 2 FREE gifts (gifts are worth about $10). After receiving them, if I don't wish to receive any more books, I can return the shipping statement marked "cancel." If I don't cancel, I will receive 6 brand-new novels every month and be billed just $4.69 per book in the U.S. or $5.24 per book in Canada. That's a savings of close to 15% off the cover price! It's quite a bargain! Shipping and handling is just 50¢ per book*. I understand that accepting the 2 free books and gifts places me under no obligation to buy anything. I can always return a shipment and cancel at any time. Even if I never buy another book from Harlequin, the two free books and gifts are mine to keep forever.

135 HDN EYLG   336 HDN EYLS

Name	(PLEASE PRINT)

Address	Apt. #

City	State/Prov.	Zip/Postal Code

Signature (if under 18, a parent or guardian must sign)

Mail to the Harlequin Reader Service:
IN U.S.A.: P.O. Box 1867, Buffalo, NY 14240-1867
IN CANADA: P.O. Box 609, Fort Erie, Ontario L2A 5X3

Not valid to current subscribers of Harlequin Superromance books.

**Are you a current subscriber of Harlequin Superromance books
and want to receive the larger-print edition?
Call 1-800-873-8635 today!**

* Terms and prices subject to change without notice. Prices do not include applicable taxes. Sales tax applicable in N.Y. Canadian residents will be charged applicable provincial taxes and GST. Offer not valid in Quebec. This offer is limited to one order per household. All orders subject to approval. Credit or debit balances in a customer's account(s) may be offset by any other outstanding balance owed by or to the customer. Please allow 4 to 6 weeks for delivery. Offer available while quantities last.

Your Privacy: Harlequin is committed to protecting your privacy. Our Privacy Policy is available online at www.eHarlequin.com or upon request from the Reader Service. From time to time we make our lists of customers available to reputable third parties who may have a product or service of interest to you. If you would prefer we not share your name and address, please check here. ☐

HSR09R

Stay up-to-date on all your romance reading news!

The Inside Romance
newsletter is a **FREE**
quarterly newsletter
highlighting
our upcoming
series releases
and promotions!

Go to
eHarlequin.com/InsideRomance
or e-mail us at
InsideRomance@Harlequin.com
to sign up to receive
your **FREE** newsletter today!

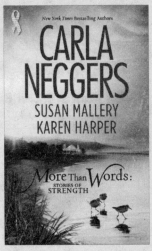
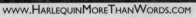

THE BELLES OF TEXAS

They're as strong as the state that raised them. The Belle sisters aren't afraid to go after what they want, whether it's reclaiming their ranch or their family.

Linda Warren
CAITLYN'S PRIZE

Thanks to her deceased father's gambling debts, Caitlyn Belle's beloved High Five Ranch is in dire straits. Particularly because the will stipulates that if the ranch doesn't turn a profit in six months, it must be sold to Judd Calhoun—the man Caitlyn jilted fourteen years ago. And Cait knows Judd has been waiting a long time for his revenge....

*Look for the first book
in The Belles of Texas miniseries,
on sale in July wherever books are sold.*

COMING NEXT MONTH
Available July 14, 2009

> ## WELCOME TO COWBOY COUNTRY

#1572 TEXAS WEDDING • Kathleen O'Brien
Just because Susannah Everly married Trent Maxwell doesn't mean she has to forgive
him. They both know the deal with this union and it doesn't include rekindling their
old love. But can she live a year with him and *not* give in to temptation?

#1573 NO HERO LIKE HIM • Elaine Grant
Hometown U.S.A.
Counting his life in eight-second increments is all Seth Morgan knows. Then a bull
beats him up in the ring. Desperate to get his body back, he takes a job at a riding
camp. All good until he falls for the boss, Claire Ford. Because he can't have her and
the rodeo....

#1574 CAITLYN'S PRIZE • Linda Warren
The Belles of Texas
Thanks to her late father's gambling debts, Caitlyn Belle's High Five Ranch is in dire
straits. If the ranch doesn't turn a profit in six months, it's to be sold to Judd Calhoun—
the man she jilted years ago. And Cait knows Judd has been waiting for his revenge....

#1575 A RANCH CALLED HOME • Candy Halliday
Sara Watson will do anything to protect her son, Ben. So when Ben's uncle
Gabe Coulter tracks them down, she can't resist his offer: a temporary marriage so
Ben can know his heritage. Once she's at the ranch, it feels like the home she's always
wanted.

#1576 COWBOY COMES BACK • Jeannie Watt
Going Back
Now that his rodeo career's kaput, Kade Danning has nowhere to go but home—
if you can call it that. After hitting rock bottom, making amends is easy. But convincing
Libby Hale to trust him again is harder than anything he's faced—in or out of the ring.

#1577 KIDS ON THE DOORSTEP • Kimberly Van Meter
Home in Emmett's Mill
John Murphy is a solitary man. Until he finds three abandoned little girls on his
doorstep. He doesn't know anything about how to take care of kids! But he takes in the
munchkins and vows to protect them—even if that means saving them from their own
mother!